THE ROCK STAR'S HAPPILY EVER AFTER

POPPY FORBES

This book is a work of fiction. Any references to historical events, real people, or real places are used fictitiously. Other names, characters, places, and events are products of the author's imagination, and any resemblance to actual events, places, names, or persons, is entirely coincidental.

Edited by Jenny Sliger of Owl Eyes Proofs & Edits

Formatted by CPR Editing

ISBNs:

978-1-990253-10-2

978-1-990253-09-6

BISAC : FIC027020

FICTION / Romance / Contemporary

❀ Created with Vellum

Dedicated to the people who have supported me most. Also, to you, for reading this and for loving these characters as much as I do.

1

CAROLINE

I hear rummaging in my kitchen from my bed, but I can't seem to move. I know that my five-year-old daughter is more than likely making a mess in the kitchen. Still, even though my brain is willing me to wake from my fog, I can't get my body to respond.

"Mum?" I hear her ask in a whisper from my doorway. Lottie's feet pad into my room, but I still don't open my eyes.

"Yes?" I ask, my voice still thick from sleep.

"Can you make me something to eat?"

"Sure, I'll be there in a minute." I finally open my eyes as my daughter runs out of the bedroom. The room is in complete disarray, and I look around till my eyes land on the lump beside me. My husband is dead asleep, unaware of the world around him. Knox Bryan still looks as good as he did when we met. His unruly brown curly hair is spilling over his pillow as I run my hands through it.

"Oh, that feels good," he murmurs with closed eyes.

"Yeah? You know what else would feel good?" My hands run from his hair down to his chest.

"What?" His inhale is sharp.

"If you make our daughter some breakfast so I can sleep." I smile as he cracks open one of his grey eyes.

"I can't believe how lazy you are." Knox pulls me into his chest.

"We got off tour literally twelve hours ago. I can barely open my eyes."

"Think about how I feel? I had to put on a show last night."

"You've been doing it for so long though that I figured in your old age that you were used to it." My husband is in one of the biggest alternative rock bands in the world, The Hestons, not to mention he is one of the best songwriters.

"Oh, you're going to pay for that." In one flash movement, Knox has pinned me below him and is tickling me.

"Stop!" I say in between laughs.

"Say how much you love me and how sexy you think I am."

"Fine! I do, and you are!"

"By the way, I'm only thirty-four." He lays back down beside me and props himself up on his side.

"That's still four years older than me. How do you feel about last night's concert?" I ask while pushing a curl out of his face.

"Meh. It was all right. I only have two weeks till we have to get back on the road." He sighs. "I can't believe you're both not comin' this time."

"I know." I snuggle closer to him.

Being married to someone in a band is less than ideal when you want to have dinner with them every night, but we both love being on tour. When we met, I was a guitar technician for the band opening for The Hestons. By the time I was twenty, I was the tour manager of a different band. Our schedules were so hectic the first few years we were together, we were lucky to spend three consecutive days together. Our relationship was always a struggle, but we managed to make it work and got married. When I had Lottie, I quit my job to go on tour with Knox so he could be around Lottie as much as possible. But when the job offer had come to take over as a tour manager for one of the biggest bands, I couldn't help myself and jumped at the opportunity.

"First time in five years I'm not going to have my girls with me."

"Knox. It'll be fine. We have a plan, remember?"

"I don't want you to be on tour with them."

The band I'm now working for, The Talons, have a less than stellar reputation. Knox wrote their newest hit single and produced a few songs for them, so he knew exactly the type of guys they were.

"I'm sure it'll be okay," I say, trying to be positive.

"They're a bunch of British assholes with too much money and too young and stupid to see what they got. Did you see the news about them last week? The two were caught in a bathroom with a girl at a club."

"You realize we live in London and are surrounded by British assholes, right? Come on! You can't tell me that Danny hasn't been caught in the same situation."

Even now, Knox's drummer, Danny Baxter, still manages to light up the tabloids with his outrageous behaviour.

"Danny is an idiot." Despite himself, Knox smiles.

"He really is. Babe, Rick asked me to come help whip them into shape. He said they're on the verge of breaking up."

When one of my best friends, Rick Schaffer, took over as the band's manager, he called to ask me to go on the tour.

"I don't want anything to happen to you or Lottie." Knox interrupts my thoughts.

"Honey, did you just meet me? Do you remember me as a tour boss?"

"I know. You'll be fine. And I know you won't let anything happen to Lottie. I'm gonna miss you both so much." He kisses my forehead.

"Well, I'm not going to miss you at all. In fact, what's the name of the super cute one that has girls going crazy for? Mick?" I smile.

"You suck." He laughs and pulls me in for a long kiss. He starts to move his hands from my hip upward. Our kisses almost become desperate as he pulls me as close as possible.

"Mummmmmmmmy?" I hear a little voice call from down the stairs.

"Damnit," Knox whispers as he pulls away.

"Coming sweetie!"

"Friday. You, me, hotel room. I'll get Candice to take Lottie." Knox grins.

"Your sister probably has plans for Friday night. She's newly single."

"She doesn't have plans," Knox scoffs, "She's a newbie to London. How many friends can she have at this point?"

Candice Bryan is a gorgeous twenty-four-year-old woman who could light up any room she entered. Until recently, she was dating Felix, Knox's guitarist, for the past two years, but she had called it quits. Knox isn't thrilled his baby sister had crushed his best friend's heart, but there were things he didn't know about their relationship, and it's best he be kept in the dark about them.

"Well ask her. If not, we can get a babysitter or something."

"Who knew having a kid would be a complete cock block?" He says and I punch him in the shoulder.

"I'm going to make our daughter some food. Come join us when you feel up to it." I slide out of his arms.

I head down the stairs and let my fingers run over the walls. Our house is nothing fancy, though we have enough money to live somewhere bigger, this felt more like our style. We did make sure to get a place with gates and trees to keep out unwanted guests. From band admirers to paparazzi, it felt like we couldn't move without being stopped by someone when we lived in St James. Knox's past is tattered with bad decisions, and most of the time people are waiting for him to backslide. Even though our house is in Primrose Hill and still in Central London, I always wanted to raise my kids here.

I kiss my daughter on the head as she continues to watch TV. I get to the kitchen and make her breakfast. I drop off her eggs before going back to clean up my mess. I hear my husband greet my daughter before he enters the kitchen.

"I spoke to Candice, and she can take Lottie on Friday." He grabs an apple and leans against the counter.

"Lottie will love that." I gaze at my husband. Even leaning against the counter, Knox's 6'4 stature is evident. I look closer at his face and notice his scruff is a little longer than usual and the wrinkles around his eyes are a bit more pronounced.

"What?" He asks, his mouth full of apple.

"Nothing."

"Sure. I bet you're thinking how much you're going to miss me. Or how much you want to ravish me right here in this kitchen."

"Yes I am." I pour myself some coffee. "Not the ravishing. I'm going to miss you. The sex is all right."

"Is that so?" He wraps his arms around my waist from behind. I can feel the length of him grinding into my ass.

"You can't do that with our child in the next room." I suck in a sharp breath as his lips make contact with my neck.

"We could if you keep quiet." His hands move from my waist down towards my centre. I'm wearing thin pyjama pants, and it's almost like barely wearing anything at all.

"Stop it. We both know neither of us is quiet." I hiss as one of his hands cup my breast, and he gives it a little squeeze. I push him away even though my body is on fire.

"Maybe I should cancel the rest of our tour so we can have more moments like this." He shakes his head in what looks like an attempt to forget what we are doing.

"You definitely can't do that. Danny, Pete, and Felix would start calling me Yoko."

"Maybe Lennon had a point for picking love, especially if they had sex like we do." He kisses the back of my head. Knox and I have chemistry that is out of this world. While there were many things we had to overcome in our relationship, sex isn't one of them. In fact, sex with Knox is enough to make me forget my own name, and at times, I did. But that was also before we had Lottie. Now, we are lucky if we have sex once a week.

"You act like I'm leaving you for good." I sit down at the kitchen table, and he joins me.

"Who knows, maybe you will." He tries to hide his smile, and I roll my eyes.

"You're an idiot."

"An idiot whom you love." He laces his fingers with mine.

"I have to head to rehearsals this afternoon. Can you drop Lottie off at daycare? I'm sure she's dying to see her friends."

"Sheesh. She loves them more than her dear old Da." His Irish accent is always a little stronger when he says 'Da.'

"Can you blame her?" I smile as Knox turns on the TV in the kitchen. I read the newspaper on the table and get lost in a story about a missing dog that was reunited with its owner.

"Uh, Car? You might want to pay attention to this." Knox turns up the volume as I shift my attention to the screen.

"Sources say that The Talons' lead singer, Mick Davies, was arrested last night for allegedly starting a fight with another club-goer. No news yet on if he's been released or if he did in fact, start the fight." The screen then flashes to pictures of Mick yelling at someone and a bunch of people rushing around them.

"Caroline. This is bad."

"What?" I ask, even though I know what he means.

"No way you're going. And no way is my 4-year-old daughter going."

"Come on, I know you don't remember the early days, but you were crazy when we met, and I don't even want to know what you were like before that." I cross my arms.

"Do you not remember the three times in rehab it took me to kick my habits?" He counters, and I try to hide the pain that still sits in my heart.

My perfect husband and perfect life weren't so perfect in the beginning. Knox's cocaine and drinking problem when we met were all-consuming and I almost lost him so many times I couldn't keep all of them straight. When I was eighteen, twenty-one and twenty-five, I had the same conversation with him; that he either clean up his act or we were done. People called me stupid for sticking through the first two visits to rehab, and by the third, I had lost all my friends and my parents. Our first year of marriage was rocky, with me being on a different tour than him, he kept falling back into old habits. When I found out I was pregnant, I told him he had one choice: to kick it for good because our child wasn't going to watch him kill himself.

"We need to have this conversation upstairs, or else Lottie could hear us, and I do not want to explain rehab to a five-year-old." I say to him and down the hallway. I tell Lottie we're going to our room and to shout if she needs us.

The second I shut the door, Knox starts in on how he doesn't want us to go because it's unsafe. I try to reassure him, but it doesn't matter, he's already made up his mind, and he isn't interested in hearing whatever I have to say. While our marriage is great, there are moments with Knox where it feels like it's final when he makes a decision.

"You're crazy if you think I'm intentionally putting her in danger with my job. My voice is shaky. I want him to realize I'm never going to put our daughter in danger. I sit on the edge of our bed and hang my head in my hands. This is going nowhere, and I'm trying not to cry.

"I never said that." He sits beside me.

"No but you implied it. You telling me I can't go is an indication you don't trust me when I've never done anything to shake your trust. I've put my career on hold for the past four years to follow you around the world. Can't you see that I need to do this?"

"I know you do. I know you need to feel like you're more than just a mom even though to Lottie and me, you're everything. I'm scared."

"Are you scared about us leaving or the fact that you'll be on your own again?"

"Both. Since the last time I got sober you've always been there." He wraps his arm around my shoulders.

"I know but you have come so far Knox." I lean against his shoulder.

"I love you and Lottie so much. I don't want anything to happen again." He rubs his face with his free hand.

"No groupies," I say as Knox bursts into laughter.

"Gross." He shakes his head. Over the last five years, I have built a relationship with Knox that's filled with honesty and love. Even with our past, I trust him more than anything. Still, groupies were always around, and they weren't going anywhere, even as we get older. The number of times we've gotten to our hotel room and naked girls are waiting for him, not knowing I'd be there, is astonishing. Not only that, but the paparazzi are also relentless. Any time Knox is with another woman, no matter who it is, you could almost bet there will be a story.

"Leave those for Danny and Pete."

We sit in silence for a moment till Knox turns to me. "I have to ask you a serious question."

"What?" I meet his gaze.

"Hear me out. What if I take Lottie with me? She knows the crew and us. It might be easier for you so you can focus on the tour."

It took me a minute to absorb what he's saying. Even though I didn't want to admit it, he's right. Lottie knows the crew and how things went with The Hestons. While Danny and Pete are down to get with any groupie, she wouldn't be exposed to the same things she might see on tour with The Talons. Not only that, but Knox would also be so focused on taking care of our daughter, he wouldn't have time to get into trouble of his own.

"You'll have to get a nanny because I do not trust any of those crew members with our daughter during the show."

"You're okay with this?"

"I'm sad, but it does make the most sense. Plus, you're right. She knows everyone on that tour."

"I'll make sure we see you every chance we can." He kisses me hard.

"You better. I need to get going. I have no idea what to wear either." I say as I notice the time on the alarm clock next to our bed.

"I think you should wear the Johnny Cash tank top with the leather jacket.

"Oh, do you?" I laugh.

"Yeah, that's the girl I fell in love with. Pinky blonde hair, lip ring, nose ring, Ramones tee, ripped jeans. Be still my beating heart." He grasps his chest.

"Becoming a mum and wife is a total buzzkill for my image." I look in the mirror at my short white-blonde hair. I still have the lip ring, but it's a diamond stud versus the hoop. The nose ring had come out, and the pink hair had gone out of style.

"At least wear the leather jacket."

"Good call. And I'll take it off and show off my tattoos, so they know I used to be cool." I have a few tattoos on my forearms and some on my back. Knox didn't have any. "I need to get in the shower."

"Okay." Knox stands up and takes his shirt off.

"Don't tempt me," I warn. My husband half-naked is enough to make me late on any given day.

"Oh, I'm coming with you."

"No way. Our kid is downstairs."

"I want to finish what we started this morning." He wraps me up in his arms and trails kisses down my neck.

My body floods with heat as Knox's fingers trail down to the hem of my pyjama pants.

"Lock the door," I mumble, and he sprints to the door to secure it.

Hot hands travel under my clothes, and I'm so turned on already that I want to skip to the good part. But Knox would never. I knew well enough; he wants to make me beg for it. It's like a dream, but I'm awake and wiggling with anticipation as Knox pushes me back on the bed. His breath is hot on my thighs as he pulls down my pants.

"No panties. My favourite." He mumbles as I slide my hands through his hair.

I feel the press of his tongue on the part of me that is already sensitive at the thought of him. He pulls my hips up and settles his mouth at the burning part of my desire. He kisses and licks the aching flesh, and I grab the pillow to put over my face to stifle my reaction. The world kaleidoscopes into incredible colours as I come apart in his mouth. I feel like a pile of mush as Knox removes the pillow from my face and lays a kiss on my lips before taking off his clothes.

"I know we do this a couple of times a month but remind me that we need to do this more often, especially if you're going to do that." I grin up at him as he tugs my shirt off.

"Sure thing baby. Good thing we can be as loud as we like at the hotel on Friday. I love when you scream my name."

I don't have a chance to respond as he kisses me hard. I bite his bottom lip, and his eyes grow dark with lust. He pins my hands above my head and presses into me about a centimetre, making me quiver.

"Don't tease me," I say, breathless.

"Tell me what you want." He whispers into my ear before sucking on my earlobe.

"I want you inside of me."

I lift my leg and hook it around his hips. I feel the hot press of him at my centre, and I'm practically salivating. Knox doesn't hesitate and slips inside of me. I'm so wet that there's no resistance, and he groans with pleasure.

"Fuck Caroline." He takes a sharp inhale.

His tempo starts to increase, and with every thrust, my body responds with pleasurable tremors.

"You feel so good." He says in-between straining breaths.

"Oh Knox." I bite my knuckles to keep myself from being too loud.

He is always uninhibited in bed, and our bodies are meant to fit together. I gasp and moan as we race toward the finish line, both aware that we really don't have that much time to drag this out.

"Come for me." He says, and my world explodes.

Knox thrusts harder, and I come undone as he does the same. I bite my bottom lip to keep the sounds of pleasure from erupting out of me. He collapses on top of me, and I can feel the sweat on both of our bodies. I wrap my arms around him, and he doesn't move.

"I fucking love you." He says as he rolls to the side and lets a hand run absentmindedly over my stomach.

"I love you too. I would love to go for round two, but we have a kid, and I have to work." I smile and kiss him again.

"Right. We have responsibilities. Remember when we spent the entire day in bed in Florence?"

"We didn't really see Florence because all we did that entire trip was have sex. I still think it's the best trip I've ever been on." I get up and head towards the bathroom. "Go check on our daughter. I need to shower."

"Right." He gets up from bed, and I admire his bare ass as he slides on a pair of sweatpants.

God, I'm going to miss him.

2

KNOX

Spring in London is here. After a particularly dreary few months, the sun is extremely welcome even with the coldness of the morning. After kissing Caroline and Lottie, I left to walk to the studio. The beauty about living where we do is the proximity to everything I need. The exhaustion seeps into my bones. I'm getting too old to be going on world tours, and this one seems to be more of a struggle than the others. When you're eighteen and want to sleep with groupies, do a ton of drugs and be up all-night partying, it's the best. When you're a dad and a husband, as well as a recovering addict, it's a lot harder. The rush of the stage is still one of my favourite feelings though.

Pushing through the doors of the studio, the smell of espresso hits my senses. I may not be able to have a beer but damn, if coffee isn't the next best thing. My feet carry me to the kitchen as if they know all on their own that I need caffeine.

"Hey man," Felix Norton, The Hestons lead guitarist and my best friend, greets me. He's wearing his typical black t-shirt with blue jeans. For someone who doesn't ride a motorcycle, he seems to wear motorcycle boots constantly. His colourful tattoos are all on display, and his black hair is a bit of a mess. His eyes are bloodshot. Whether it's from drinking or crying, I'm not sure. Felix and my sister, Candice, dated for the last few years, but recently, she called it off. Felix has been nothing short of a wreck ever since.

"You look horrendous," I say to him as I make myself an espresso.

"Good to see you too," Felix snorts.

"You know as your best mate; I'm goin' to give it to ya straight." I move around the small kitchen, grabbing water to fill the back of the coffee machine. Felix takes a seat at the round table.

"It's the same shit every day now. Feel sad, get drunk. Get drunk, then feel sad. I don't know how to get through this. No bird has ever left me before." He lets out a sigh.

"Candice will come to her senses. She's going through a phase. You remember being twenty-four? Any sort of settling down would be terrifying." I take a sip from the cup.

Felix shifts in his chair but doesn't reply. There's something about their breakup that they're not telling me, but I don't pry. When they first got together, I told them both I'm staying out of it, and if they broke up, I wasn't taking sides.

I lean against the counter, and we sit in silence for a few more moments.

"What's up fuckers?" Danny Baxter, our drummer and other best friend, says as he joins us.

Felix, Danny, and I all grew up together in Northern Ireland. We found our love for music early and hit up the Belfast live music scene as much as possible. Felix and I took guitar lessons starting at nine, while Danny said in order to get the most chicks, he was going to be our drummer. After a few years of practicing nearly every day, we finally had a break in a small pub in London. It had been one of the few gigs we did outside of Northern Ireland, and it had been the best thing we had ever done. At that show, we were introduced to Callum Mattis, our band manager, and the reason we're able to be professional musicians. Callum said even if we hadn't met him, The Hestons still would have been mega-famous, but I don't think that's true.

"Looks like you didn't go home." I smirk. Danny is wearing the same post-show clothes he was wearing yesterday, the signs of a good night.

"Naw mate. Met up with some chicks who were at the show. Admit it

Knoxy, you miss the life before marriage and kids." Danny grins and takes a sip from the bottled water he grabbed from the fridge.

I stroke my chin, pretending to contemplate his comment. There's absolutely no way I miss life before Caroline and Lottie. If it hadn't been for Caroline, I'd be dead. There's no doubt in my mind that I would have ended up in a gutter, and all of this would have turned out differently.

"I don't miss it one bit. But that does remind me. Caroline and I agreed that I'm going to take Lottie with us on tour. At least for the first part so Caroline can get her bearings with The Talons." Even saying their band name makes my blood boil. The thought of my wife around that idiot Mick for an entire ten-month tour makes me want to pull my hair out. She can handle herself; I just wish she didn't have to. Thankfully I'll know Lottie will be safe with me. Or maybe I'm thankful for the responsibility to keep my idle hands busy.

"Ah right. So guess we'll have to keep a clean tour again." Felix shoots Danny a look.

"Hey! I never do anything around the Bryans. I'm smarter than that," Danny says.

"Another thing, I will have a nanny with us, so neither of you can shag her." My eyes connect with Danny's because, really, he's the only risk.

"Hire an ugly bird then." Danny chuckles.

Felix shakes his head, and I laugh. Danny heads out of the kitchen to go to his space at the studio. For me, the best thing about being in The Hestons is being able to afford our own studio, where we record with only the people we want to. Not only that, but we also have our own offices that sometimes double as bedrooms, depending on how the album is progressing. We also have a space at the back that we can rehearse when we're not on tour. This is our own rock star sanctuary.

"You gonna tell me how you feel about Caroline going on the road with The Talons, or do I have to beat it out of you?" Felix eyes me.

I let out a breath and place the mug of coffee on the counter. "It's mostly selfish, honestly. Caroline's good at her job, you remember."

Felix nods.

"But what if shite goes south? What if I end up…?" I can't bring myself to say it.

"It's been years Knox. There's no way that's going to happen. You aren't the same person."

"It took me three times to kick the coke habit. It's not hard to imagine that I could slip."

"You could. Or you could remember all the things that you have. Plus, you have us. Danny is a bit crazy, and there's zero chance of him ever-changing. But we're getting a bit old for all the shit that comes along with the road. I can hang out with you and Lottie. Keep you on the straight and narrow. Don't worry." Felix stands and puts his hands in his pockets.

"Thanks, mate. I appreciate that." I give him a small smile.

Felix gives me a pat on the back and then heads out of the kitchen.

It's easy for anyone who's never had an addiction problem to say that. To tell me things are going to work out. Except what they don't know is the underlying issues or what exactly the drugs were covering up. Felix and Danny never seemed to have the same problem as me. They could have a night out, get completely obliterated, and then they're fine. They don't continue to binge for days until they're so depressed that they can barely move.

I rub my face. It's selfish of me to think that Caroline didn't have dreams outside of our household. It isn't fair for me to expect her to come on the road with me every time I tour but she is the only person who keeps me grounded. She's the only person who sees me as I am—a flawed man—not some big-shot rock star. And that's why she deserves to do something bigger than being my wife.

A few hours into the studio session, my brain is stuck. Danny has created the perfect drumline for a song that we've been trying to finish for weeks. Felix has nailed the intricate guitar parts. But I can't seem to write a lyric to save my life. I should have never given *My Amazing Girl* to The Talons. They have done incredible things with it, but it's about my Caroline. Those lyrics were written at the beginning of our world tour before I had any idea what the song was going to be. She had been taking care of a sick Lottie and after getting our daughter to bed, instead of looking after herself, she had gone backstage and ensured that everything was set for me. Caroline's always doing that. Ensuring that everyone in the world has things before she does. The song is completely Caroline's and when she told me I should sell it to The Talons, I knew then she was doing it for one of her oldest friends, Rick Shaffer.

"I gotta go pick up Lottie." I put down my pen. The blank page is staring back up at me—taunting me.

"Okay man. No problem. Maybe tomorrow the song will flow ya know?" Felix says.

"For sure. It's probably a bit of a foggy mind since getting off tour." I nod. I stand from my chair, and Danny and Felix wave at me before I head out the door.

Next to Caroline, no one in this world can replace Lottie. She's the funniest little lass, and I still don't know how I got so lucky to have a daughter like her. Lottie's daycare is a block away from the studio, another perk of our neighbourhood.

"Dad!" Lottie calls from the courtyard. There's a white iron fence that encloses the area. The red brick building emulates a school building. Children are buzzing around, running up to the playground, or chasing each other. My little blonde curly-haired daughter is too enamoured by my appearance to notice any of them.

"Hello, love." I smile down at her. Lottie's eye colour matches my own, but everything else is all Caroline.

"Can we go home?" she asks.

"Of course. Do you have your bag?" I look around and give a wave to Gloria Marchand, Lottie's minder, and she nods in return. Lottie grabs her Paw Patrol backpack and runs to the gate. She rockets into my arms after it opens, and I squeeze her.

"Missed you, Dad," she says into my shoulder.

"Missed you too, dolly."

These moments make all the hard shit worth it. I drop her back to the ground, and she grabs my hand while I carry her back in my other. I notice people staring at us, nothing new, but it bothers me when I'm with Lottie. She didn't choose this life; she shouldn't have to be subjected to everything that comes along with fame. Though at five, she's mostly oblivious to it.

"What do you say we make mum something nice for dinner?" I ask and Lottie beams at me.

"Yes!"

"What do you think she'll like?"

"Uhm maybe macaroni and cheese?" Lottie taps her chin with one finger.

"That sounds like Lottie's favourite dinner, not mum's." I wink at her, and she giggles.

"She does like it Dad. She told me!"

"Okay, okay. We can make that. I think we have everything at home we need. Are you going to help me or watch TV?"

"Maybe TV," she says, and I laugh.

We continue to walk with Lottie singing random songs she's made up. She gets that from me. I wonder if she's going to follow in my footsteps and momentary panic flutters across my chest. I now know what my parents meant every time they sat me down for a chat about my drug abuse. There's no way my daughter could go down this path. The thought vanishes when Lottie stops at the edge of our house.

"Shall we go inside?" I ask her before I punch in our gate code. Growing up in a small town outside of Belfast, there was never any need for gates, but in London with our high profile, I'd do anything to protect my girls.

"Dad, are you going to miss mum when we go back on tour without her?" She asks.

It's an astute observation for such a young girl. We assume Lottie is never listening when we talk around her, but clearly, she has been.

"Of course, I am," I say. The gate opens gradually when I type in the code. I usher Lottie inside, but she moves slow.

"Me too." Lottie stares down at the ground.

"You know we're going to see her as much as we can, and we can Face-Time her every night." I crouch down, so I'm at her eye level.

"All right Dad." Her face says she's not convinced and I'm having a hard time persuading myself.

"But Uncle Felix is going to be there. That'll be fun, right?" There is no one in this entire world Lottie loves as much as Felix. I wish I could say it was Caroline or me, even Candice, but no. She loves the rocker with the black hair and tattoos. It's a foreshadowing of my life to come as she starts to date in her teens. If I have any say though, she won't ever date.

"Yes!" She cheers and then sprints to our front door.

Unfortunately for me, having Felix on tour isn't as big of a sell. I love the guy, but he's not my wife.

3

CAROLINE

The first step out of my car at the rehearsal space causes an overwhelming need to go back home to build in my stomach. Rick spots me from the front door and waves. Damn. It's too late to turn around now. Rick doesn't have an inspired wardrobe and usually sticks to blue jeans and a black golf polo. He's recently waxed his shaved head, and as the sun bounces off it, it almost blinds me.

"There she is!" Rick's British accent floats towards me on the wind. I grab my backpack and head towards him.

"How long has it been?"

Rick pulls me in for a hug. "Too long. Follow me to your temporary office."

"Thanks." I smile.

"The guys are all going to come in one at a time to meet you. They're looking forward to meeting you."

"Great. That sounds more ominous than you intend, I'm sure."

He strides ahead of me and stops at a closed-door with my name on it. It's nothing fancy but seeing Caroline Harper-Bryan in permanent marker on the door makes me giddy. This is exactly what I need. I love being Knox's wife and Lottie's mom, but there's a part of me that feels like it's ready to bust out into the world again.

"Is Mick out of jail?

"Ah. You saw the news this morning." Rick sighs. "He's out but not here yet. He'll be in an hour, according to his bodyguard."

"He's a peach huh?"

"Reminds me of Knox back in the day."

"Don't you dare say that! He was never a dick to anyone." I shake my head.

"You don't remember the first tour you did with them." Rick eyes me. Rick and I met on the first tour I ever worked on. Rick was a roadie for The Hestons.

"As I recall, we all did a ton of drugs back then and were all jerks." I remind him.

"Yeah, but Knox was entitled and stuck up," Rick says.

"I'm going to agree with you, but you can never tell him that I did."

"I would never do such a thing!" He laughs.

"How's Chuck?" I ask.

"He's pissed I'm going on another tour. He thought I would retire one day." Chuck is Rick's boyfriend.

"You're only forty!" I say.

"Yeah but forty is like eighty in tour years." Rick stops in front of a solid wooden door. When he opens it, there's a small dark wood desk, and a black chair tucked into it with another chair on the opposite side. There are calendars on the walls and what looks like outlines of important tasks —whoever had this office before me had been organized.

"I should tell you that Lottie isn't coming with us anymore." I move inside the room and place my bag by the chair before pulling it out and taking a seat.

"What? Why?" Rick asks.

"Knox pointed out that maybe for my first tour back, it wouldn't be a great idea, and she already knows his crew and bandmates." I look down. I know it's going to be painful without my daughter.

"Well shit. I was hoping to hang out with my Goddaughter more. Are you all right with that?" he asks.

"Every time we have more than one day off, I'm going to try to fly to see them, and Knox is going to do the same. We'll make it work. We always do," I reply.

"You can't bail on me halfway through!"

"I would never. Unless I can't stand the guys." I smile, and Rick takes a seat across from me.

"Then you might as well leave now." He places two hands on the back of his neck and whips his feet up on my desk.

"Are they really that bad?" I ask.

"Did Knox not tell you?" he asks.

"Well he gave me the cliff notes," I say.

"I guess we will see what you think. I'll send the first one in," he says.

"Okay. Can you make sure Brandon is in the middle? I heard he's the nicest," I ask.

"Good idea," Rick says as he leaves my office. I open the computer and look at the budget for the tour.

After three hours of meeting with the first four guys, I've gotten a handle on who they all are. Conner seems sweet enough, making sexual jokes as much as possible and Tommy doesn't seem to really know what's going on ever. Kane is quiet and Brandon is as lovely as Knox described. Now it's time for the worst one. *Mick Davies.*

An hour goes by, but Mick still hasn't shown up to my office. I text Rick to see if he can send him my way so I can start prepping more for tour. My phone starts to buzz, and I see Knox's name flash.

"Hi honey," I answer.

"Hi love," he replies.

"How's it going at the studio?" I ask.

"Great. Laying down some tracks for the new album. I think this might be the best one yet," he says.

"How many songs did you write about me this time?" I tease. Knox says that all his songs come from our experiences.

"Only a hundred. I'm really cutting it back." He laughs. "Have you heard the lads play 'My Amazing Girl' yet?" My Amazing Girl was the song Knox wrote for The Talons that went to number one a few months ago.

"Not yet. I can't wait to hear another man singing a song about me to me." I laugh.

"I'm glad I didn't keep that song. I couldn't sing it without choking up every time." Knox wrote the song after Lottie was born and had sung it to me only once.

"I remember. I think I cried the entire time too. I'm sad you didn't record it, though. You singing it would have been much better."

"True. Tonight, I was thinking pizza and a movie? How does that sound?" he asks.

"Extremely perfect."

"Great. Then I think we put Lottie to bed, throw on some Barry White and make out a little."

"Oh you know the way to getting my pants off." I giggle. "I gotta go. Love you."

"Love you too." Knox hangs up.

I recheck my watch and start to type out some initial plans for merchandising. I get lost in my own world and feel an intense gaze land on me.

"Mick. Come in." I get up and motion for him to come inside. I hold out my hand out for him to shake and smile. He looks at my hand and sits down without saying anything.

"Okay," I say and sit in my office chair again. "How are you feeling?"

"Fine." His answer is brief, and awkwardness hangs in the air between us.

"Are you looking forward to kicking off the tour?" I smile and he narrows his eyes.

"Sure. Where are you from? American?" He asks.

"No, Canadian."

"Interesting. Look, let's not get in each other's way. I know the reason you got this job is because of your husband, so do your job, and we won't have a problem, okay, sweets?" He's patronizing me.

When my eyes connect with his, there's fire in them. "First off, never call me sweets. Second, my husband most definitely did not get me a job that will take me away from him and my daughter for ten months. He actually likes having me around. Last, I got this job because I have worked on many tours."

"Many tours? You look maybe twenty-four. How many tours could you have possibly done?"

"I'm thirty. If this is the foot you want to start off on, then fine. But you're not going to get rid of me by being a dick. I've handled my fair share of assholes in my career, and you're another one I can deal with."

"So, Miss Priss has a bit of bite. Perfect. You're going to need it because you're not going to last. You're tough now but wait."

"Miss Priss? Wow. Tell me something. What's it like?" I ask.

"What?" He frowns.

"Being so far up your own ass." I cross my arms.

"It beats having a stick up it," He shoots back and stands up. "I'm out of here. Tell Rick I'm leaving."

"You have to rehearse." I stand in protest. *No, no, no Caroline! This can't be the way the first day ends.*

"Guess you can tell them you pissed me off, and this is your problem now." He shrugs and heads down the hallway back to his dressing room.

I sit down and let my head lean back in defeat. Even though he's a prick, I didn't want our interactions to be terse, but here we are. I pick up my phone and dial Candice's number. She always knows what to say and I need her to come over for a pep talk tonight.

"Hi, Caroline." Her sing-songy Irish accent greets me. I can hear bar sounds in the background but that's not surprising. Since Felix and Candice broke up, that's a common place for her.

"Hi, love. Are you free? Why don't you come over for dinner? Lottie would love to see you, and honestly, so would I after the day I've had." I let out a breath.

"Sure. I'll scoot home and then come over around five-ish?" She says.

"Sounds good! See you soon." I click off and smile. I'm so glad my best friend lives in London.

Today has been bad at best, and the sweet relief of my home is in sight. I cannot wait for Knox to give me a hug and Candice to threaten to beat up Mick. She's the best for that. I get in my front door and sink a bit against it. *Can I really do this?*

"Car?" I hear Knox call to me from the living room.

"Yeah, it's me," I say back.

"Come here for a minute, would ya?" he says.

"Coming," I call back. I walk down the hallway and look at our pictures on the walls. A part of me is starting to regret this decision. I walk into the room, and my hands fly to my mouth. The room is bursting with colour from all the bouquets. Lottie is wearing a dress and grinning at me. Knox has set the table, lit candles, and put on a tie. My husband doesn't wear a tie.

"What is all this?" I ask as Lottie wraps her arms around my legs.

"For you, mummy." She looks up at me.

"For me? Why?" I look at her with tears in my eyes.

"Congratulations on your first day, my love." He walks over to me and kisses me.

"What did I do to deserve you?" Lottie unwraps herself from me and sits down at the table while I pull Knox in for a tight hug.

"No, my dear. The question is, what did I do to deserve you?" he smiles.

"I love you. So much," I whisper into his neck, not breaking the embrace.

"I love you more," he answers and rubs my back.

"How was the studio today?" I ask as I take a bite of my pizza.

"Good. We're almost done with all of the guitar tracks." He takes a drink of water.

"That's amazing."

"How was your first day?" Knox asks. Lottie is standing up, trying to see the TV.

"You can sit in the living room but be careful not to spill," I say to her, and she smiles at me before she takes off.

"So much for a family dinner." Knox's eyes glimmer, revealing the teasing nature.

"Now we can talk, and she won't drop her plate on the floor," I reply.

"Good point. Back to how your day was," he says and takes another bite of pizza.

There's a knock at the door before I can respond. A bemused expression crosses Knox's features.

"Candice," I say and stand.

"Ah." Knox nods.

I let Candice in, and Knox doesn't quiz me any further about my day, probably for the best. I don't need to add stress to his life.

After dinner, Lottie is still lost in TV land, and Knox goes back to the studio. Candice hugs him, and I kiss him before he heads out.

"Come sit." I place a teapot and two cups down on the coffee table. Candice sits beside me while I pour her a cup.

"So today was bad, huh?" She asks and takes a sip of tea.

"I don't know how to describe it, Candy. He is such a dick. I thought going back to touring would make the passion I've been missing come back, but I feel burnt out, and the tour hasn't even started." I fiddle with the cup's handle.

"Caroline, you're going to be brilliant! There's nothing I'm more sure of." She smiles at me and places her hand over mine.

"Thank you for saying that, even though I don't believe you. Mick is trouble Candice. He's mean and surly— I can't believe he's caused so much shit within The Talons. The band is basically on the verge of breaking up. No one likes each other, and Mick is the cause of it all. He has lead singeritis." I take a long sip of tea and place it back down on the table.

"What?" She laughs.

"When a lead singer thinks he's better than his band, it's basically the beginning of the end. It's a partnership. One, unfortunately, many lead singers forget."

She nods.

"I think Knox is worried about going on tour alone." Saying it out loud to someone else helps the weight I've been carrying on my back to lift slightly. There's something in the way he looks at me, a worry behind his grey eyes, screaming the pain of what could happen if he relapses again.

"Why? He's come so far. There's no way he's going to go back to the old Knox." She frowns.

"I know. He worries is all." I look out the window then back to her. "Mick seems like a mini-Knox, the one I used to know. Maybe that's why I'm so worried about working with him."

Candice nods, and her eyes look a bit glazed over as if she's retreated somewhere in her brain. If anyone knows what I went through, it's her and her family. It's been such a long road and the thought of Knox reverting is almost enough to get me to quit this tour. With Mick's constant bad attitude, well, that might send me over the edge.

4

KNOX

The phone in my hand burns a bit as I debate whether to call Felix or not. He has always been the first person I call, but he doesn't seem like the right choice this time. I dial a number I used to know so well and listen to the dial tone as it rings. *Maybe he won't pick up.*

"Knox? It's been a while." Roberto's voice still has a slight Spanish accent.

"Don't worry. I'm not in any trouble, mate." Jokes come so naturally for me.

"That's good to hear. Still not sure why you'd be calling your sponsor, whom you haven't talked to since the last time you debated relapsing unless…" He stops.

"I'm not going to relapse—at least I don't think. There are so many things going on in my brain right now. When you left the industry, how was that for you?" I ask. For a while now, I've been considering stopping touring all together. But the thought of telling Caroline feels difficult.

"The great Knox Bryan is thinking of retiring?" Roberto chuckles.

"Caroline is going on tour with The Talons. The road without her seems bleak."

"Always a poet."

"Honestly, though. Didn't you get sick of the late nights and all that? Isn't that why you quit?" I play with the microphone that's sitting in front of me.

"I quit because I couldn't stay clean. You've managed to stay sober for the last five years, and things seem to be going quite well. Is this all tied to Caroline?"

His question hits me in the gut. Of course it's not. Caroline and Lottie are a large source of happiness for me. But when I'm alone, and the thoughts of doubt and pain seep in, it's hard to block it out with deep breathing.

"Maybe." I bury those feelings again. They tell you that you have to tell people about your pain in rehab, but I'm tired of doing that. I'm tired of having people look at me like I'm going to make a mistake again.

"If there's more to it, you know you can tell me."

"I know."

"Go home. Hold your wife and your baby. Count your blessings," Roberto says.

"Good call. Thanks—for everything. I don't know where I'd be—if you weren't my sponsor and friend." I rub the back of my neck. When it comes to feelings, outside of my songs and Lottie and Caroline, it doesn't come naturally.

"Wow, you really struggled with that one." He laughs. "No problemo. You can always call."

We say our goodbyes, and I place the phone down. I pick up my guitar and start to write. It'll help me get out of this funk.

I stroll into my house around 9 PM, hoping my sister went home and my daughter is asleep. Normally, I love being around both of them, but I have plans for my wife. Plans that involve being extremely naked. Caroline is doing the dishes in the kitchen, and I wrap my arms around her waist and kiss her neck.

"Please tell me Candice is gone." My breath fans across her neck, and she shivers.

"Sure is. She's going to be back early tomorrow though. I think she's lonely." She dries her hands before she turns to face me. She wraps her arms around my waist, and I hold her closer—*ten months of not holding my wife every day.* I shake my head at the thought. She's here right now, and I need to take advantage of that.

"I have something for you..." I let go of Caroline and pull a small box out of my pocket.

"What is it?" She asks as I hold the box out to her.

"Open it."

She opens the box, and a gorgeous, huge, square-cut yellow diamond with small white diamonds haloed around it stares back at her.

"Knox," she whispers.

"I know you love your wedding ring." I pause and run a finger over her simple diamond band. "But I want to make sure people realize that you're taken." I take the box back and slide the ring over her finger.

"I love it." She wraps her arms around my neck.

"I love you."

"I love you too."

"If Mick continues to be a dick to you, I'm going to struggle with not being there."

"That's a random thought after giving me a beautiful present." She chuckles.

"I mean it, Caroline. I'm not going to let some jerk be mean to you for no reason. He's a stuck-up little..." She cuts me off by placing a hand over my mouth.

"Now listen to me. I'm going to be okay. I'm strong and I love how much you want to protect me, but this world is filled with mean people, and you can't save me from all of them."

That's my Caroline. Always a spitfire. The toughest woman I know, honestly. She's been through hell with me, she doesn't need any more.

"I know, but I want to." I lean my forehead against her.

"And I love you for that too."

"Can I play you something new?" I let go of her and she leans against the kitchen counter.

"Absolutely."

"Mummy?" A small voice calls from up the stairs.

"Coming Lottie. Hold that thought." Caroline winks at me and heads up the stairs. I go into the living room and grab my guitar.

Caroline shuts Lottie's door, her footsteps light as she heads back down the stairs. I have my Gibson Vintage Hummingbird acoustic guitar in my hand, absentmindedly strumming the chords, waiting for her. Caroline grins when she gets to the doorframe.

"Come to me." I stop strumming and hold a hand out to her.

"You are such a dork." She giggles and hits my hand playfully before sitting beside me. God that laugh can bring any man to his knees.

"Don't tell anyone. It might ruin my rock star image." I strum the chords again in the same pattern to match what I created in the studio earlier.

"Are you going to sing to me?" She asks.

"Absolutely. I think you'll like this song."

"Okay go!"

"My, my, my, what do we have here?" I sing and stare at my fingers, ensuring I remember the chords. "A crazy girl with little fear. She took my hand, and this I swear, she told me she'd never leave. I love her more than she knows. I'll love her till the day I go. Her emerald eyes deep-rooted in my brain, and her smile, her smile makes me go insane." I strum the guitar and pick up the beat a little. "You my girl are the one and only, you my girl fulfill me wholly. No matter where you go, I'm going to love you until the end of my time. You give me so much, and stealing my heart was your biggest crime." I stop and take a moment before I make eye contact with her.

"I love it." Her smile is wide.

"It's not done, obviously." I rub the back of my neck. I could play this song for millions of people but playing it for my muse causes me to feel stripped bare. She's the only person who knows me inside and out.

"Well, it's fantastic."

"It's about you."

"No way really?" she says sarcastically.

"Shut up." I laugh and place the guitar on the ground. "How come you haven't written anything in a while?"

Many people don't know how much help Caroline has been

throughout my entire career. In addition to being my muse, she's been my writing partner when there's a song that's not quite sounding right. She's an incredibly talented guitar player, but she doesn't think so.

"Because writing songs is more your thing. I can play the guitar," she says.

"You are good at writing songs." I lay down and pull her into my chest.

"No, baby. You are good at writing songs. I'm good at being in them," she murmurs into my neck, causing my entire body to tense with pleasure.

"True. I don't know how I'd write a song without you." I kiss her.

"While I love that you think that, but I know for a fact that you don't need me to write a good song," She starts to play with my necklace, her fingertips causing goosebumps with every contact on my skin. This woman drives me mad. No woman can do to me what Caroline does.

"I'm not ready for you to leave." I sigh and kiss the top of her head.

"Me neither. I'm scared I made the wrong decision." Her voice is quiet.

"You did. You aren't going to be able to stare at my sexy arse the entire tour." I tease her.

"I have a pretty good picture of it in my mind." She pauses. "How many cheating rumours do you think we'll start? Or break up rumours?"

"At least once a week, I'd say," I say—the downside of being in the public eye. There's never been a doubt that Caroline is my only one and has been for the last twelve years but try convincing the public. I can't even walk near a woman without a story about how I'm a cheating bastard.

"Make me one promise." She tilts her head up, and our eyes connect.

"Anything," I say.

"Tell me everything. The good, the bad, everything." She looks away and fiddles with the chain around my neck once more.

"What are you gettin' at?" I frown. She can't possibly think I'm going to cheat. Not after all this time and not with the rock-solid foundation we've built. Our life together isn't something I'd trade for anything.

"Nothing specific, but I want to know everything and I'm going to tell you everything. I don't want there to be any lack of communication between us because that's when trouble will start." She shrugs.

"Okay. Everything. Should I be worried about anythin'?" My mind starts to race. There's something she's not saying, as if she knows about my call to Roberto earlier. It's not that I don't want to tell her about it. I just don't want her to worry.

"No. Should I?"

"No. We've come too far to ruin this now." I shake my head.

"Agreed," she says. "I love you."

"I love you too," I say. "Now let's get you naked."

Caroline's hands are like fire as they move up and down my torso. She pops the button of my pants and then slides them along with my boxer briefs down my legs.

"I said get you naked not me." I chuckle.

"I can stop." She winks, and I grab her hands to stop her from pulling off my pants. Her tongue comes out, wetting her lips.

I pull her t-shirt above her head, and I almost die when I notice she's not wearing a bra. My fingers brush over her nipples, and her body quivers. I bite my bottom lip; nothing is hotter than turning her on.

She pulls her jeans and panties off quickly and pulls me on top of her on the couch. I take my shirt off. Our lips meet, and our kisses become desperate as our tongues meet. I deepen the kiss, and I flip Caroline so she's on top, straddling me. I sit up slightly, wrap an arm around her back, and pull her close, so she doesn't fall. My hands are moving up and down, over her hips and her ass. She rocks against me, and my erection starts to get painful.

"God, Caroline," I mumble into her neck. My hands come around to cup her breasts, and my thumbs rub against her nipples before I take one of them into my mouth. Caroline moans slightly, and all I want to do is be inside of her. I intertwine my hand in her hair and tilt her neck to the side so I can pepper it with kisses.

"Knox." She moans. She lowers herself onto my cock, and it takes all my effort not to explode right away. Caroline makes me feel like a teenager every damn time. I flip her onto her back and push into her, filling her completely. Her pussy is so wet for me. Our bodies are made for each other. Every inch of me fits perfectly.

Caroline digs her nails into my back, and the sensation spurs me on to go deeper. My thrusts become more sporadic.

"Knox, I'm going to come. Come with me." Her voice is a whisper. We're trying to keep quiet with Lottie upstairs. Her muscles tense around me. As her panting and whimpers start to come out, she bites her hand to keep quiet. I spill every last drop into her, and I rest my forehead against hers.

"Holy shit," I whisper.

"Do we keep getting better or?" She giggles and wraps her arms around me.

"We're like wine, baby. We get better with age." I smirk, and she laughs.

"You are a dork, but I love you." She smiles.

"I love you too. So much," I say.

5

CAROLINE

B*uzz. Buzz.* My phone vibrates on the nightstand beside me, and I open my eyes to look at the clock. 3:30 am. *Who the hell is calling me this late?*

"Hello?" I mumble. Knox stirs beside me.

"Car?" Rick's voice is on the other end. "I'm so sorry for waking you."

"It's okay," I wake up a bit more and yawn. Knox is wide awake and staring at me. "What's up?"

"It's Mick," Rick says.

"Oh?" I reply.

"Yeah, he got himself into some trouble tonight. He's not getting charged or anything, but I was hoping you could pick him up from the police station. Chuck and I decided to go out to his parents' house for the night, so I'm about two hours away, I'm afraid," he says.

"Doesn't he have people for that?" I ask.

"It seems as though they're all busy," he says.

"Uh yeah, I guess I can do that then." I sit up.

"Thanks, Caroline. You're amazing." He hangs up before I can respond.

"Fuck." I breathe.

"What's going on?" Knox mumbles.

"Sorry. I have to go get Mick from the police station." I sigh and pull on some yoga pants that were lying on the floor next to our bed.

"Seriously?" Knox replies.

"I know."

"I'm coming with you."

"Lottie."

"Caroline, this kid is going to be the death of you," he says.

"People said you were going to be the death of me too at one point." I walk around our room, looking for a hoodie to throw on.

"This isn't the same. You go there, drop that prick off at his house, and get your ass back here. If you're not back in two hours, I'm coming for you," he says.

"I know. Go back to sleep." I kiss his forehead quickly and head down the stairs—time to get the prince.

I pull up to the police station, and the place is swarming with paparazzi. *Great.*

I slide my sunglasses on and put up my hoodie. Like that's going to make a difference.

"Caroline Bryan?" Someone calls my name as soon as I get out of my car. I don't say anything and soon enough, the paparazzi are snapping photos of me.

"Are you here for Mick?" a woman shouts.

"Are you and Knox over?" a man asks.

I push past them and make it inside.

"Ms. Bryan?" I hear from behind me. A young police officer is staring at me. He looks to be about my age.

"Yes."

"I'm a huge fan of your husband," he says, and I smile. "You're here for Mick?"

"Yeah. Is he around?" I ask.

"This way. We kept him in a cell. He was a bit riled up," he replies.

I see Mick sleeping on the bench in a cell. "Thanks, Officer…"

"Officer Howard." He finishes for me.

"Thank you, Officer Howard," I say, and he walks away. I turn my attention back to Mick.

"Oh, hey Caroline," he opens his eyes sleepily.

"Get your ass up. We're leaving." I cross my arms.

"I'm quite comfortable here," he says without moving. I walk over to him and hit him.

"Get up," I hiss through gritted teeth.

"Fine fine. I'm up. Where's Rick?" he asks and sits up.

"He's away," I say. "Don't you have a bodyguard or something to get you out of this mess? Are you going to tell me what happened?"

"Nope." He walks past me, and I follow him.

"There are a ton of paps outside."

"Where did you park?" He scans the sea of paparazzi.

"Through the crowd." I sigh.

"Shall we?" he asks.

"I guess so." I pull my hoodie up and put my sunglasses back on. We get to my car relatively untouched. A few of them asked if we were dating and it takes all my effort not to puke.

"That was fun," Mick says.

"You look like hell," I say. I jam my key into the ignition, and the Black Range Rover roars to life.

"Thanks, babe. You look right fit too," he grabs Knox's Ray-Bans and slides them on.

"Remember to give those back," I say. "Where do you live?" Mick grabs his phone.

"Shit. I can't go back to my place. My other security guard said that the place is swarmed," he says. I feel a twinge of empathy for him. Every time Knox would get out of rehab or when I was pregnant, we would have to hire a full security team.

"Where am I dropping you?" I can see him starting to fade.

"I don't know. Anywhere." He closes his eyes, and he's out.

Damnit. I stop at a light and know where I have to take him.

I pull into my back driveway, where we're sheltered from any photographers. I drive straight into the garage and shut the door as soon as possible. Mick is still sleeping.

"Wake up." I shake him.

"No," he mumbles.

"Wake up, kid." I shake him again.

"Where are we?" he asks, looking around.

"My house," I reply.

"Why are we here?" he says.

"Where else are you gonna go? I'm not going to let you sleep on the street. It's bad for business." I undo my seatbelt, "Come on." Mick does as he's told for once and follows me into my house.

"Nice digs," he says as he looks around.

"You can sleep in the guest room. Don't wake up my daughter or my husband…" I say.

"Caroline?" I hear from behind me. Knox stands in the doorway of the kitchen. *Shit.*

"Hey honey." I smile then stand between him and Mick. The last thing that we need is a row that'll wake up my daughter.

"What the hell is he doing here?" Knox's voice is low.

"The paparazzi have his house surrounded. He had nowhere else to go," I whisper back. Mick is staring at our family pictures.

"I'm going to show Mick to the guest room. You stay down here." I place my hands on Knox's chest, and his body relaxes a bit.

"I'll be down here when you're done." Knox turns and goes back into the kitchen.

"Ooo you're in trouble." Mick chuckles when I reach him.

"Follow me." It's the first time Mick's right. I'm for sure in trouble.

As soon as I open the door, Mick kicks off his shoes and flops onto the bed. It doesn't take more than a second till he's passed out. I walk slowly down the stairs towards my angry husband.

"Hey, babe." I smile at Knox. Maybe if he remembers he loves my smile, the scolding won't be too bad.

"Don't you dare."

Shit, he's seen through me.

"This isn't good, Caroline." Knox sits on the couch and runs a hand through his hair.

"I didn't know what else to do. He reminded me so much of you at that time, and I felt sad for the guy," I say.

"I get it, but he's an asshole. He's got an end game. There's no way it's a coincidence that he ended up here," Knox says.

"You act like he's this crazy mastermind. He's a complete idiot!"

"Just you wait. That kid is a selfish prick. There is something up his sleeve. I've seen it before with his type... hell I was his type for a while."

"I'm sorry," I move towards the couch. I sit and wrap one of my arms around his waist.

"Yeah yeah." He lets out a breath.

"I am." I reach up and twist one of his curls around my finger.

"You haven't even been working for them for a full day, and we already have an asshole rock star in our guest room." He looks up at me.

"It's been a rocky beginning," I agree. "Let's go back to bed."

"There's no way I'm sleeping while that kid is still here. I'm going to go for a run. I'll be back in a bit," he says.

"Okay." I sigh and walk upstairs. Knox is right. It has been one day, and Mick was already causing me problems at work and now at home. This better be worth it.

The light streams through the blinds, and I momentarily forget the commotion from last night. It sounds like Knox and Lottie are downstairs, chatting in the living room. I slip into some sweatpants and throw on a jumper. Hopefully, Knox burned off his annoyance with his run. This isn't a new thing for him. The second there's stress or pain or anything remotely upsetting, Knox goes for a run. He's exchanged his drug high for a runner's one, and I'm grateful for that.

I get down the stairs in time to see Candice walking through the front door.

"Hi Caroline." She grins at me.

"Thank God you're here… It's been a crazy night." I lean against the wall as she starts to unlace her boots.

"Why? What happened?" Candice balances as she pulls one boot off.

"Oh—" Before I can finish my sentence, Knox joins us.

"Candy." Knox nods.

"Knoxville." She nods back.

"Do not call me that!" He chuckles.

I let out a breath of relief. Maybe things are going to be all ri—

"Candice. Lovely to see you again." Mick strolls down the stairs, moves past me to grab Candice's hand and kisses it. She looks temporarily stunned as her head bobs back and forth between the three of us.

"Uh, yeah," she says.

"So, you do know my sister?" Knox's gaze narrows at Mick.

Does Mick know Candice? How?

"Yeah, I told you." He winks back at Knox. It only takes a second for Knox to have Mick pinned against the wall.

"You're dead!" Knox shouts.

"Stop!" I grab his arm and push in between them.

"We don't actually know each other," Candice cuts in. "We met for like twenty minutes yesterday."

"You prick," Knox says as my hands press against his shoulder. "You led me to believe it was more."

"I can't help what you assumed. You know what they say about assuming." Mick laughs wickedly. Knox tries to move past me, but I hold my ground.

"Okay. You need to go in here." I push Knox to the living room. "Candice, can you show Mick out?" I ask.

"Sure. Hey arsehole, come with me." Candice motions for him to follow her to the back.

Knox walks past me and up the stairs. "I need a minute before we can talk about this. On second thought, maybe go to work, and we can talk about it when you get home."

"Sure." My stare follows him till he's out of my sight.

I let out a breath then head to the kitchen. After brewing a cup of coffee, I pick up the paper. There's noise coming from down the hall.

Lottie and Knox have migrated to the living room. Candice walks in and walks over to the coffee machine.

"Can I have some?" She asks me.

"Of course, my love." I smile. Candice is my saving grace right now.

"You're the best," she says. "Aren't you going to be late?" She takes a seat across from me at the kitchen table.

"I've got time. Rick said it'd be okay if I was a little late, seeing as how I was up at three-thirty."

"Ah. Yes. Everything all right?"

"My husband is pissed. I had a dickhead rock star in my house that is definitely up to no good. My life is great." I give her a sarcastic thumbs up.

"I'm sure Knox will get over it. He's not as tough as he looks," she says. She does a bit of a sideways glance around my kitchen. I know immediately she's thinking of her place in Belfast. Her entire life has changed so much, and here I am complaining over work shit. She doesn't need that piled on her too.

"You're right about that." I nod. "So, Mick?" I need the details. How had he known Candice's name? Were they a thing?

"Nothing is going on."

"I never said there was." I hold my hands up.

"I went out with Nadine yesterday afternoon. She's into his friend Tommy—"

I cut her off. "Tommy? Really? Wait, aren't Nadine and Danny a thing?" Nadine isn't my favourite person. She has been a bit wild, making Candice a bit wild as well. But she's been there for Candy, so I can't be upset by that.

"Not really. I think they were only fooling around. Does Danny ever settle down?" She raises her eyebrows. There's one thing everyone knows about the drummer for The Hestons, it's that Danny Baxter is never going to be a one-woman kinda guy. The things I've seen him do with girls while on the road—the memory causes a shiver to go down my spine. He's definitely an exhibitionist. Thankfully he's toned it down since we started bringing Lottie on the road.

"True. Okay, continue, please," I say.

"He was trying to lay some lines on me, so I got up and left."

"You walked out on Mick Davies? Who are you?" I burst out laughing. "I mean, I definitely would have done the same thing, but wow, I'm so impressed."

"He's a douchebag. After I got your texts yesterday, I was pissed, so no, thank you. It's not like I'm hard up for douchebag rock star boyfriends." She lets out a sigh.

"Don't let Lottie hear you say that," I say. Lottie has an obsession with Felix. "How are you doing since the whole break up?" It's a stupid question, but I don't know how else to check in on her. She's been struggling, it's obvious, but I've been trying to be there for her as much as possible.

"It sucks. I miss him, but it's for the best. He needs to figure out how to be a good boyfriend who doesn't cheat on his girlfriend." She shakes her head. "And getting married at this age sounds awful. I realize you were married and pregnant by my age, but I'm not you."

"I get it. I love Knox and Lottie, but sometimes I wonder what it would have been like to have my twenties free to do whatever. Not like I can complain though. I've seen the world a few times over, and I'm extremely lucky. And I agree Felix needs to get his shit together," I say. My eyes follow Candice's gaze as she looks at the photo from our wedding day. The best day in the world, in my opinion. No matter how mad Knox is right now, there's no doubt that he's the man I'm supposed to be with. He'll get over this. It's one of those fights all couples have. At least, I hope it is.

"You are. Plus, you have a great best friend like me." Candice grins at me.

"You are the best perk I could have gotten." I squeeze her hand. "So, tell me my eyes were deceiving me though when I was looking into my backyard and saw you leaning in while Mick whispered into your ear?"

"I went temporarily insane. You can't deny that he's pretty."

"So pretty. So pretty I hate myself for saying it." I groan. Mick Davies is gorgeous. I'm not blind, but the arrogance makes his beauty only a mask for the ugly underneath.

"I wish I could get away from the UK for a while. Everything here reminds me of Felix."

"Are you going to take your necklace off?" I ask.

Her hand immediately touches the white gold cross Felix bought for her birthday. "Eventually."

We sit in silence. I take a sip from my coffee. I wish there was some way for me to get Candice out of this funk—especially since I'm leaving for a world tour for almost ten months with few off days. I wish she could come with me. The loneliness of the road is going to kill me without Lottie and Knox.

My face lights up, and I slap the table. "Okay. I have an idea but tell me if I'm crazy. Come on tour with me!"

"Are you serious?" she asks. "Doing what?"

"We need a new hairstylist! You might be the answer to my prayers because begging everyone else was really the only plan I had. One rule though."

"Sure! Anything!" She smiles.

"No Mick." I give her a stern look. I swear I see her face fall, but she recovers quick.

"That won't be a problem."

"Great! This is going to be amazing! I'll talk to Rick the second I get to work," I say.

"Talk to Rick about what?" Knox asks as he enters the room.

"Caroline asked me to go on tour with her," I smile.

"Oh, did she now?" He grabs a cup from the cupboard.

"Yup! Okay anyways. I'm going to go find my niece. Ta, my dear," she says to us.

My husband's eyes narrow as she flounces out of the room. He's ready to grill me now, and I can see in his face; he's not impressed.

Oh boy.

6

KNOX

"You invited Candice on tour? With that asshole?" My blood is pumping. *Calm down, Knox.*

"I figured it'd be good for her to get away. Things with Felix and all have been terrible." Caroline shrugs, but it doesn't make me less mad.

"Caroline, I don't want my sister around that." I shake my head.

"It's not your decision. It's hers. She's not a little girl anymore." She gets up and places her coffee mug in the kitchen sink. "I get that you're mad at me but don't make Candice pay for that."

I let out a sigh. I'm not angry at her per se. This situation is already fucked, and she hasn't even left the safety of London. "I'm not angry with you, Caroline. I don't know what to do. I'm scared."

She turns to face me. "I know you are. So am I. But we can't take it out on each other."

Tell her Knox. Tell her about the dark cloud that's hanging over you.

"I know." I nod. I've never kept anything from Caroline, but the last thing I want to do now is take this away from her. "You have to promise me though, that you're going to talk to Rick about this. This is dangerous."

"Knox, I get that Rick is our friend, but he's also my boss. I'm not going to start complaining about the job when it's been one day."

"You're going to let it go then? Pretend it didn't happen?" My heart is thumping. "That's really dumb."

"Thanks. I'm going to get ready for work. We can talk about this more later."

I reach for her, but she moves out of my grasp. I don't say anything and watch her go.

"Knox we're going to head out," Candice calls from the front entrance.

My mind is berating me as I walk towards the door. I smile down at Lottie. She wraps her arms around my legs. My daughter is the best thing that I've ever done. I reach down and pick her up for a hug. She looks so much like her mother but with my eye colour. Lottie squeezes me, and I drop her down. I say goodbye to Candice and shut the door after they leave.

Instead of going to talk to Caroline, I grab my stuff and head out to the studio. I need an escape.

After a few good hours at the studio, my mood has lifted. Danny and Felix had left to go meet up with some groupies. I swear I heard Felix call Candice earlier, but he'll never admit that to me. It's hard not to pry, but I love them both, and I want to keep it that way.

"Knox?" A woman's voice calls behind me.

"Lena. How are you?" I ask. Lena Baros walks towards me and takes a seat next to me in the production booth. Lena has been the general manager at our record label for the last five years. She's originally from Greece, and her black hair and tanned skin reflect that. She always wears a pencil skirt and white button-up. Danny calls her the naughty librarian, and it's obvious why. Both Felix and Danny have tried to take her out, and she's turned both of them down. Her husband is a respected cardiologist in London. She's one of my and Caroline's favourite people and we've had many dinners with her and Harry.

"Yeah, good, thanks. And you?" she asks. Her face says otherwise, though. Come to think of it, Lena hasn't been to my studio in months and usually gives me a heads up she's coming. Something is going on.

"Your face says otherwise." I eye her carefully.

She lets out a breath and crosses her legs. "Look, the album is running long."

"I know." I swallow hard.

"I heard Caroline isn't coming on tour?" She asks.

Fucking Danny. Can't keep shit to himself.

"She's not. But that's all right. Lottie is coming with me."

"That's great." She pauses. "You know how much I adore you and your family—"

"Get to it, Lena." I don't need her to draw out what I already know she's going to say.

"The label is worried that you're not going to finish this album in time. I'm worried that without Caroline, there might be some old—" she stops. "—habits that might come back."

"Lena, come on. I'm clean. I wouldn't do that to Caroline or Lottie. You know that."

"I do, but you know that I have investors I have that need to be reassured that their star isn't going to go off the rails. We can't have you leaving the tour early either. There's a lot of money at play here." She gives me a tight smile.

"Right. That's all I am here, a money-making machine. I feel like I've made the label, investors, and you a lot of money so far. Don't worry, your cash cow isn't going anywhere." The words are harsher than I intend. This label has given me everything, and Lena is my friend. The dirty side of this business always gets to me.

She winces. "Knox, you know I'm doing my job. The album is already six weeks late. That's not normal for The Hestons. You're usually done early."

"There's a few issues with inspiration for the lyrics. The lads are done with their parts."

"I know."

A silence hangs between us then something clicks in my mind.

"They called you?" I ask. My fucking bandmates—no, brothers—ratted me out?

"They're worried about you. You haven't been the same recently."

So people have been noticing. I figured I'd been hiding it so well. The fact that dipshit Danny and emotionally unavailable Felix have noticed then it must be worse than I initially realized.

"I'm fine. It's a lot of change in a short period. I'm trying to adapt." The lies come so easily. No one needs to know about the growing depression. No one needs to know that it's not only Caroline leaving but that it's been building for months now. I can't let my wife down.

Lena nods. "I understand. It has been a big month for your family. Remember that we are always here for you. Whatever you need."

"Thanks. Actually, can you set up some interviews for a nanny for Lottie?"

"We can arrange that. I'll get my assistant to do the preliminary interviews, then send the best you and Caroline's way."

"Thanks."

"No problem." Lena stands. "Before I go, we do need the new album by the end of the month. You go back out on tour in two weeks. You need to get this wrapped up so we can go into production and plan the marketing strategy."

"Understood." I nod.

"Good." She smiles. "Please text me any time. Not only about the album. You and Caroline are family to Harry and me."

"I will. Everything's good," I say.

She gives me one last glance before ducking out of the studio.

The lyrics in my notebook are staring up at me. Nothing seems good enough. Caroline liked that one song I played her yesterday, but that's not even close to finished. There's nothing in this book that's going to be near as good as our past songs. I need to outdo myself, or I get torn apart by music critics. The first record after I got clean had such mixed reviews that I swore I'd never let it happen again. One reviewer said that they wished I was still on drugs because that's where my creativity clearly came from. There was a time I believed that too, but the album after that had done so well that it pushed that thought out of my brain. I don't know how I'm supposed to write about love and life when all I feel right now is darkness.

I dial Roberto's number again, and he answers quick. "Hey, I'm good. I need your help with something. Meet me in an hour at the coffee shop—"

I hang up. Maybe there is a right option in order to move forward.

7

CAROLINE

Knox left without saying goodbye, which made a pit form in the bottom of my stomach. Something is going on with him, but I can't bear to ask what. If it's cocaine again, I don't know if I could survive that. I push that aside as I get up from my desk. As I walk the hallways towards Rick's office to talk about Mick, my plan is to give him a brief overview of the night before but ensure he doesn't think that I'm complaining. I knock lightly on Rick's office door.

"Hey lovely!" Rick greets me as I step inside. I take the seat across from him.

"Hi! How were Chuck's parents?" I ask.

"Old." He winks, and I giggle. "What's up?"

"I was wondering if it would be all right if my sister-in-law, Candice, could come on tour with us? She won't get in the way and can help with anything that needs doing. She is a trained hairstylist," I say.

"What about Felix? Is he going to let her go?" Rick asks.

"They broke up actually."

"Really? It so happens that we need a hairstylist. Get her to come in tomorrow."

"Thank you!" I say and stand.

"Anything to keep you happy," Rick smiles.

With one more thanks, I leave and walk down the hallway to my office. When I get to the door, there's a note attached to it.

Miss Priss,
Meet me in the rehearsal space now.
Mick

I throw it in the trash. *What a dick.* I walk into the space to find Mick sitting with Tommy.

"Leave," he says to Tommy. Tommy doesn't say anything and walks out.

"Am I in trouble or something?" I ask.

"Nope. Just a friendly chat." He smirks and sits on the edge of the stage.

"How come when I think of friendly, you don't come to mind?" I cross my arms, keeping a distance from him.

"I'm nice sometimes."

"I'm not giving you Candice's number."

"How did you know that's what I was going to ask?" He frowns.

"Because you're see-through," I say.

Mick jumps off the stage, getting closer to me. Before he can say another word, the door opens behind us.

"Can I help you with something, mate?" Brandon stands between us.

"Nope. Enjoying a chat with Caroline here." Mick breaks his stare on me to glare at Brandon.

"Looks like this conversation is over," Brandon says. Mick turns on his heels and stomps out of the room.

"Thank you," I say. "Although I had it under control." The last thing I need is to be the reason these two really kick-off.

"I know you did, but he can be a little unstable sometimes."

"I'm surprised he never hit you," I say and sit down. Brandon grabs one of the acoustic guitars from the stage.

"Mick would never hit me. We may hate each other now, but we were best friends once. Maybe the closest out of everyone."

"No way. I don't believe it." My mouth drops, and Brandon sits beside me.

"This is going to blow your mind then. We used to live together."

"What? Okay, now I must hear your guys' history," I say as Brandon strums the chords lightly.

"I've known Mick since I was ten. He became my best friend pretty quick, and we were inseparable. We took guitar and drum lessons together. Then Mick started to sing, so we decided to try to get a band together. We met Tommy through mutual friends, Conner responded to an ad we posted, and Kane was someone we met through school. We were so close. He was my brother, but he's changed a lot." He sighs.

"I've seen that happen a lot. Weird thing is that as people get older, they usually change back to the good version of themselves—sometimes," I say. Knox would be one of those people. He changed for the better, and I'm so proud of him.

"I'm not saying he's a lost cause, but I'm not totally sure he'll ever be my friend again." Brandon starts to strum harder.

"Whatever you're playing sounds great." I change the subject.

"Oh really? It's something I've been working on," he smiles.

"Are there lyrics?" I ask.

"Yeah," he blushes.

"Sing it to me."

"I don't know, Caroline. I'm not much of a singer. I mean, I can carry a tune, but I'm not as good as Mick." He continues to play.

"I doubt that, but I'll try not to judge. Knox always plays what he's working on for me. I've been told I'm a great person to bounce songs off of." I smile.

"Okay, okay. If you promise not to tell any of the lads, I'll play it for you," he says.

"Why not tell the boys?" I ask.

"Mick only wants to play songs he writes. Your husband's song is the first one that we've played that he hasn't written," Brandon says.

"Really?" Now I know why he hates Knox so much.

Brandon nods. "Yeah. The label said we needed to change it up a bit so that's when they asked Knox for a song. Mick was pissed."

"Well then. I'm glad it went to number one then." I smirk.

"All right, but if it sucks, know that I warned you," he plays the chords louder. "Close enough, far away, I wish that you could have stayed. You knew me better than most. You and me we've been coast to coast. You taught me things I never knew, but you told me things that were untrue. You were my best friend, till the end. Losing you was like losing the sun; now I'm ready, ready to run. Betrayal, lies, my friend you're the cause of your own demise. One day, one day, I want you to see, that you, you really hurt me." He plays a few more chords after he stops singing then finishes.

"Brandon, that's amazing," I breathe.

"Come on, Caroline. It's okay, but nothing amazing." He scratches the back of his head.

"I'm serious. I'm texting Knox. You are going to play this for him." I grab my phone and text my husband quickly.

"Thank you!"

"Do you mind me asking who it's about? It's kinda nice to hear a song that's not about me."

"Uh, it's actually about me and Mick's friendship," he says. "I know it's kind of weird to write a song about an ex-friend, but I write what I feel I guess."

"Not weird at all. Knox writes songs all the time about different situations. It doesn't always have to be a love song or an unrequited love song," I smile. And my phone buzzes with Knox's reply, "Knox wants you to go by the studio and play it for him!"

"That sounds awesome. Thanks, Caroline."

"Of course. I'm glad to help," I reply. Brandon is a talent that needs to be nurtured, and I'm going to ensure he gets to where he deserves to be.

The next day I'm waiting for Candice. Her interview is today, and I'm a bundle of nerves.

"Caroline?" Knox calls to me from the kitchen. Last night had been awkward. We barely interacted, and when I went to bed, Knox stayed up late, so I was already sleeping when he came to bed.

"Yeah?" I ask.

Knox comes out of the kitchen and walks to me. "I know we argued, but I think we need a night away from here still."

"From our house?" My eyebrows scrunch together.

"Yeah, I think we need—we need to reconnect without any distractions and talk about everything before you're gone." Worry crosses his features.

"Knox, what's going on. Are you all right?" I ask, searching his face for any hint of what it could be.

"I'm fine. I don't want to fight. I want to love on you before you go." The worry is gone, and he smiles.

"I'll make sure Candice is still game to watch Lottie Friday." I reach up and push back his hair. He wraps his arms around me and pulls me tightly to his chest.

"I love you," he whispers.

"I love you too," I say into his neck. I take a deep inhale of his scent, and he smells like black coffee and his cologne. "I am going to go to the office. Our daughter is upstairs in her room freaking out because she can't go to the studio again with you today."

"I'll deal with it." He leans down and kisses me before letting me go then slapping my butt.

"Frisky this morning." I giggle.

"We haven't had sex in two days. That's too long." He winks.

"Agreed." I lick my lips, and Knox groans.

"Get out of here now before I throw you over my shoulder."

"Love you." I laugh and get outside.

Candice is walking up the driveway as I get outside. She's holding two coffees, and she hands me one when she gets closer.

"I love your outfit!" I say.

"It's okay?" she asks.

"Very appropriate." I nod.

"This is why I love you," she says.

We hop into my eighty-four Mercury Comet. It was a present from Knox for my twenty-fifth birthday. He's always been one for over-the-top gifts. Being from Canada, this is the car I learned how to drive in Britain, which is a whole different driving ballgame.

"God, getting out of the house today was ridiculous. Lottie was pitching a fit about not going to the studio with Knox," I say and start my car.

"Why can't she go to the studio today?" she asks.

"Knox is having trouble finishing the song, and he said he needs the quiet today—which is fair. He's been taking care of her most of the week between studio time and will be taking care of her for the next ten months, so I think a break is allowed."

"How was yesterday after?"

"Usual. Mick and I argued. Tommy and Conner played immature pranks on each other. Brandon sang me a song he's working on, and then I planned out some of the expenses for the trip."

"Why does Mick always bicker with you? I don't get it. You're like the nicest person," she says.

"Okay. What do you want?" I laugh.

"Nothing," she says. "You've already done so much for me. I love you."

"I appreciate it and I love you too. But I also know you… so what's up?" I eye her carefully. I know her well enough to know this is Felix related.

I let out a breath, "Felix called this morning."

"And?"

"And he wants me to come back to him. Do you think I made the right decision?" she asks.

"Did he make you happy?"

"Of course."

No he didn't. The number of times she cried over him, there's no way that's happiness. Did she love him? Sure. But they weren't happy. "What I mean is does he make you crazy? So crazy that even when you're mad at him you still love everything about him? Like you'd go to the ends of the Earth to make sure he had everything he needed, and you would pick him over everything else?"

She pauses. "I thought I did. But no. If I did then I would have married him."

"You'll know when you meet the one. Trust me. You wouldn't have thought twice if it was Felix. I think this showed you he wasn't it," I say.

My husband's smile pops into my mind. There's no doubt I love him more than anything or anyone except Lottie.

"I know you're right, but when he calls, it kills me to hear him so sad."

"You can't help that, unfortunately. Give it time," I say as we pull up to the building. There are a million fans out front. "Great. There's more than yesterday." I wave at the security guard, and he lets us in.

"Holy shite. This is insane." Candice gets out of the car and looks at the girls standing outside the gate.

"Yeah, the boys are a hot commodity." I laugh. I roll my eyes as a black SUV pulls up. The prince has arrived. Candice's eye is immediately drawn to him. *No. Shit.* She stares at him as he gets out of the car and walks over to the gate to chat with fans. A small smile plays on her lips, and that's when I see it. This isn't a lust thing. She's looking at him like I look at Knox. But there's absolutely no way I'm about to tell her that. Maybe if I ignore it, it will magically go away.

"Come on Candice," I call to her.

"Coming." She finally tears her gaze away and follows me inside.

"I'll show you my office and then bring you to Rick's so you can come back here when you're done."

"Thank you!" Candice says, and she's buzzing. Our doors are only a few apart, so the tour isn't long at all. I leave her with Rick and head back to my office.

When I sit behind my desk, my stare lands on the photo of Knox and me. I was only twenty, so Knox was twenty-four, and his arms are wrapped around me. I'm laughing at something he said. I was so crazy in love with him that I didn't even realize how bad his addiction was back then. Going into this tour, I'm ready for it but damn, if there's not something nagging at the back of my mind. All I can do is hope that this time, it's going to be different.

8

KNOX

I've been looking forward to Friday since Caroline, and I decided we would spend a night away. My sister deserves a present for this one. I left Caroline a note to meet me at Claridge's Hotel. Claridge's is one of the most beautiful hotels in London. Before we moved into our house, we stayed at this hotel for a week, and at that point, there was no Lottie. It was room service and continuous sex for seven days. The Corner Suite at the Claridge's had cost me quite a bit, but I'm happy to splash out for this occasion. Caroline is everything to me, and she needs to know. Roberto had given me the idea to reconnect with my wife, and I'm so glad he did. Not only is he my sponsor, but he's also the only person who knows about the feelings of depression. Telling Caroline would cause her to worry, and I don't want to do that. Not unless it becomes a real problem.

I busy myself, placing flowers everywhere and lighting all the candles the room has. Tonight is going to be perfect. I sit down on the couch and wait for Caroline. Hopefully, she'll be here sooner rather than later, as I'm bursting to put the shit of the past few days behind us. A few moments later, there's a beep at the door, and Caroline walks in. My heart nearly stops. She's wearing a tight black dress that comes just above the knee. Her blonde hair is styled straight, and the heels elongate her legs.

"Frederick VonKnox is freakin' rich." Caroline giggles when she sees me on the couch. Frederick and Lisle VonKnox are the fake names we use whenever we want to have a quiet time away. Caroline has always found them hilarious.

"He has to impress his socialite wife, Lisle." I stand and walk towards her. When I have her in my arms, I kiss her hard. When I let her go, she smiles at me then I lead her to the couch. I wrap an arm around her shoulders, and she leans into me.

"Do you remember the night we came up with Frederick and Lisle?" she asks and looks up at me.

"I'll never forget it. The same night you told me you loved me," I say. It had to have been the second-best day of my life—with Lottie being born the first. Caroline and I would always agree on that.

"Nineteen and crazy. In love with a rock star," she says.

"I think you kicked me in the balls that night." I laugh.

"You tried to make me jealous with a groupie!"

"Did not! She asked me for an autograph. I was giving the fans what they asked for." He smirks.

"Yeah, by signing her tits." Caroline rolls her eyes.

"Occupational hazard?"

"Yeah, yeah. I can't believe in one week we won't be able to do this." She sighs.

"Still time to pull out." She gives me a look, and I say, "I'm proud of you. Look, I know I may not have been the most supportive this past week, but I'm scared."

"I am too, but I know us. We've got this." She grabs my hands.

"I know." Except I didn't know. If this business has taught me anything, it's to expect the unpredictable. "I have a few more surprises."

"Knox! You have to stop doing that!" She shakes her head.

"Relax, relax. It's nothing expensive," I say, and she raises her eyebrows. "Not super expensive anyways."

"All right."

"So first thing is…" I pause for dramatic effect. "I looked at our schedule, and Lottie and I can meet up with you guys when you're in Canada."

"Really! That's amazing! For how long?" She asks.

"Only for the week. We'll go to Toronto with you as well as Vancouver—"

"No." She cuts me off.

"Car..." Vancouver is the one place Caroline hates more than anywhere else. Her parents live there, and to say their relationship is rocky would be an understatement.

"I love you, but no." She wrings her hands—something she always does when she gets nervous.

"It's been five years. You need to see your parents. Lottie should meet her grandparents."

"She has grandparents, your parents. Amazing people who have never turned their back on us." Her eyes bounce back and forth. I know immediately she's thinking of the last time we saw them. After I had relapsed again, they told her to leave me, except when she didn't, they told her to never talk to them again. There's always been a bit of guilt from my side for being the reason why they don't talk anymore.

"We will meet you in Toronto. Then you decide what we do when we get to Vancouver, okay?" I squeeze her hand.

"Thank you. I'm still so excited you guys will be there." With the memories tucked back into place, she smiles at me again.

"Good. Next surprise. Close your eyes."

"Closed." She shuts her eyes and giggles. I get up and grab the guitar case I had hidden in the corner. I place it on her lap, and her face scrunches up.

"Open them."

"Knox, you didn't." She gasps. Caroline is one of the most talented guitar players I know but she hasn't picked up a guitar that much lately.

"I don't know. Could be an empty case." I shrug. She opens the case with trembling hands, and a blue acoustic Gibson Hummingbird stares back at her.

"I—I—" she's speechless. I have scored quite a few husband points for this. "I—I love it. I love it so much." She starts to tear up.

"No crying," I say.

"I'm not crying." She sniffs.

"I want you to start playing again."

"I love you," she says and climbs onto my lap. "I love you more than anything in the world. And listen to me when I say this. It's not because you buy me things. It's because you are the most supportive, lovely man I've ever met. You encourage me, love me, and most of all, support me. Lottie and I are so lucky."

My heart almost explodes out of my chest. This woman is remarkable. "I feel the same way. I do have one more surprise."

"I don't know if I can handle it." She smiles but doesn't move off my lap. I click the play button on the remote, and music fills the room.

"Is this?" Caroline starts, but I shush her.

The slow acoustic melody plays, and my voice comes through as I sing *My Amazing Girl.*

"I recorded it for you." I gesture for her to move, and we both stand. "Dance with me?"

"Forever," she says. We sway to the song, and her body starts to shake against me.

"Stop crying, Caroline." I hold her tighter.

"I can't help it. I love it so much." Her eyes peer into mine.

"I love you so much." I bend down and kiss her.

"I love you too," she whispers when I pull back. She looks up at me with a glint in her eyes. She pushes out of my grasp.

"What?" I ask.

"Nothing." She grins and walks towards the bedroom.

"Naked?" I ask.

"Oh yeah, it's definitely time to get naked." She giggles.

I chase her into the bedroom. Nothing feels better than this, and my mind is only on her as I pull her onto the bed. This is the most intoxicating feeling.

Caroline is asleep when I pick up her guitar and start to strum it softly. There's a melody in my head I've been trying to nail down for days now. This night with Caroline has broken some of it free, now if I could only finish it.

"Are you playing my guitar?" Her voice interrupts my thoughts.

"You bet, baby," I say and smile.

"What time is it?" she asks.

"Midnight." The red of the hotel clock is illuminated beside me.

"Damn you and your night owl-ness." She pulls the sheets over her head.

"Did you say, 'night owl-ness'?" I chuckle and continue to play the guitar.

"I may have. My brain doesn't work this late at night anymore."

"Soon you'll be pulling all-nighters again."

"I used to be so good at them too, but I also had extra motivation then."

"Having sex with me was a good excuse to stay up all night."

"No offence, honey, but I don't think you've ever kept me up all night. Maybe like an hour of the night." She sticks her tongue out at me.

"Caroline Harper-Bryan! That was the meanest thing you've ever said!" I burst out laughing.

"Baby, you rock my world. Don't worry." She winks. I place the guitar back in the case on the floor.

"Come here." I pull her close to me.

"How's the album coming? I realize I've been so wrapped up in me lately that I forgot to ask," she says.

The one question I don't want to answer. "It's good…"

"The truth this time." She looks up at me. This damn woman can read me so well.

"It's not good. There are a lot of unfinished songs. A lot started though." I leave out the part where Lena came by. She doesn't need to know how bad it really is.

"That's not terrible," she says.

"It's not terrible, but you know me. Everything I touch has to be platinum." It comes out as a joke, but I'm entirely serious. I want everything to be a chart-topper, but nothing seems to be coming easy right now.

"Can you play me something?" she asks.

"I can do that," I say. She moves over to her side as I grab the guitar. I prop myself against the headboard and start to play the only melody I have finished.

"Oo, that's pretty," Caroline says.

"Yeah, the melody is done, but the lyrics are rubbish." I sigh.

"Let's hear the first verse," she says. I play a bit louder then start to sing.

"Disaster is one way to put it, you broke my heart, you shook it. I lived a life before you and I'll live one after, cause baby you're a disaster." I stop. That's all there is of this song. It's about Candice and Felix. Felix had said something along those lines when they first broke up, but it feels a bit wrong to sing about them.

"That's not a typical Knox-like song. It better not be about me," she says.

"It's not. It's about Candice and Felix. I started to write it at the beginning of their breakup, but it's hard," he says.

"Why?" she asks, and I keep strumming.

"Writing songs is easy when it's emotions you feel on a regular basis, but I'm happy so writing about heartbreak isn't my strong suit." *Happy.* It's not a lie. I am happy in my relationship, and I'm happy with her. I don't know if happy is the right word anymore, though.

"That is the sexiest thing you've ever said, and I definitely want to have more sex with you, but right now, I'm going to help you finish the song." She sits up, and the sheet pulls down a bit, exposing one of her perfect breasts.

"Can we have sex then finish the song?" I groan as my groin tightens.

"No. Let's go." She nudges my leg and throws on one of my t-shirts that sits just above her knee.

"You're wearing that, and I know you're naked underneath. How am I supposed to concentrate?" I pull on pyjama pants. They hang low on my hips and Caroline's eyes slide up and down my torso.

"You're not wearing a shirt." She places a hand on her hip.

"Yeah, but I don't have glorious breasts." I grin.

"Stop. Grab the guitar and follow me to the couch."

"Fine." I pout and follow her to the small living room with the guitar case in my hand. She sits down, and I join her.

"Now start the song over," she says as I pick up the guitar.

"Fuck, you're bossy." I smile. She's the only person who's ever been able to tell me what to do without getting an angry reply.

"Duh. Now play!"

"Disaster is one way to put it, you broke my heart, you shook it. I lived a life before you and I'll live one after, cause baby you're a disaster," I sing.

"My arms, my arms felt right, wrapped around your waist," She sings as I keep playing. "But baby, baby you move too fast pace. I couldn't hold on, you were gone and now, now I'm alone."

"Holy shit." I stop. "Where the hell did that come from?" I grab my phone and type it into my notes.

"I don't know," she says. "I felt your melody."

"We need to keep going." Why didn't I do this before? Caroline's gotten me out of a writing rut before, but I don't ever want to burden her with my shortcomings.

"Do I get writing credits?" She laughs.

"Of course," I say.

"I'm kidding."

"I'm not." I begin to play the guitar again and sing what comes to my mind. "Tell me the reason, the reason you left. Was I not enough? We built a life; we built a home. I'll let you go, I'll let you roam. You are my beautiful disaster, a dangerous hurricane, you've left me with nothing after, you've left me here going insane."

"Ooo, I like that," she says as I finish.

"Me too." I continue to strum. "I think that'll be more of the chorus."

"Verse two?" she asks.

"I'm struggling to start it." As quick as inspiration came, it's gone. I continue to pluck the chords when Caroline sings again.

"I wish you would come back, even though you left me with nothing. Cause baby, baby, we had something," I sing, "maybe it wasn't a love of the ages, but I can't seem to turn the pages. You told me I was the one, that you were done. No matter what, I'll be waiting, treading water, in need of saving."

I stop and stare at her.

"What?" she asks.

"I forgot how great you are at writing songs."

"Stop it." She hits my shoulder.

"I'm being serious. Why haven't you been writing with me this entire time?"

"Maybe because I can't really help you write songs about me, but this one isn't, so it's easy." She shrugs.

"You continue to impress me."

"I'm glad I can still impress you."

"Always." I lean forward and kiss her forehead. She is my inspiration in life, and I need to tell her that more often.

"Shall we continue?" she asks as she opens her eyes.

"Let's continue—" I stand and place the guitar into the case. "Tomorrow."

"Knox," she eyes me, and then we kiss. I need to be inside of her. I need her so bad right now.

I pick her up, carry her to the bed, toss her onto it, and then jump beside her. "I love you, Lisle."

"And I you, Frederick." She giggles as I pull her close, kissing her hard once again.

9

CAROLINE

I wake up next to my sleeping husband and push the curls out of his face. *Shit, I love this man.*

"Knox," I whisper.

"Caroline," he says without opening his eyes.

"We have to go home."

"No." He turns away from me like a child.

"Yes. Candice will need to go home eventually."

"Five more minutes." He turns back with his eyes still closed.

"Fine." I keep my eyes on him.

"I can't continue sleeping if you are going to stare at me," he says.

"Sorry." I giggle.

He opens his eyes. "You're lucky you're so hot. I think we might have time for one last roll around."

I kiss him, then lean back to rustle around in my bag. "I want to check my phone quick."

My phone screen flashes with three texts from Rick, nothing from Candice, which means my child is fine. Another work thing. Probably about Mick.

Rick: *I hope you had a good evening! Also maybe Google yourself...*

I look up at Knox, and my stomach does flips.

"What is it?" Worry crosses his features.

"Rick told me to Google myself," I say as I type my name in the Google search bar. As soon as I hit enter, tons and tons of news articles pop up. I read the top one.

"I'm going to fucking kill her," I say.

"What?" Knox says and sits up. "Who?"

"Your sister." I turn the phone to him.

"Is that?" he asks.

"Of course it is," I sigh. The picture is of Mick leaving our backyard and getting into a dark SUV. The problem is that the headline reads, 'Mick Davies leaves Tour Manager, Caroline Harper-Bryan's House in the Early Morning.' The rest of the article goes on to say that Knox was working in the studio all night and that I'm having an affair.

"How can she be so stupid?" Knox growls. He's wide-awake now.

"I told her to stay away from him," I say.

I text Rick back.

Me: *Well, that is one way to wake up. It's not what it looks like.*

"I think we need to take a few deep breaths before we get home," I say to my husband, who's currently putting on his clothes as fast as possible.

Rick: *I know. You told me that you and Knox were going out tonight, remember? The question is why was he at your house in the first place? I'm going to guess it has something to do with a different Bryan...*

"We can take a few breaths, but it's not going to change that I'm going to murder her." Knox runs a hand through his hair.

"She's probably going to be fired because Rick knows we weren't home last night, and he told her she can't sleep with any of the boys if she wanted to work on this tour," I say as I text Rick.

Me: *Maybe he was there to get the paper?*

"Good. She needs to learn that she can't keep going around snogging every rock star that hits on her," Knox replies.

Rick: *I don't think so. I'm not going to fire her, but she needs to keep her nose out of trouble... What are you going to do about the media storm coming your way?*

"Knox. Stop. It might not be what we think it is," I say. Candice can't be this dumb, can she? "Rick asked me what we were going to do about the media storm."

"I'll call Cassie." Knox's publicist is used to dealing with stories like this. "Plus, we can get someone from the Claridge's to 'leak' that we were here."

"Then why was Mick at our house? It's going to look weird," I say.

"Are you saying we pretend that we were home?" he asks.

"Yes, and that you were there too." My brain begins to turn, and I snap my fingers. "Maybe you can tweet something about how it was good to catch up with him?"

"No way." He shakes his head. "I hate that fucker now more than ever. It'd be a big lie, and we tell Lottie to never lie."

"Come on Knox... The world knows that Candice and Felix broke up. She doesn't need this to add to her plate of drama, and Felix doesn't need to think that she's sleeping with Mick." I sigh.

"I know you're right, but I want to let her drown in this. She needs to be more responsible," he says, and I laugh.

"You do remember what you were like at twenty-four, right? Come on, babe. I know you're mad, but you love her, and we're not going to let this get out of control." I walk over and wrap my arms around his middle.

"Fine."

"Who are you texting?"

"The prince himself."

"You have Mick's number?"

"Sadly yes," he says. "He has to back up the story if we want it to be believable."

"You're a good brother." I smile. Knox's relationship with Candice is one of the reasons I fell in love with him. He's always been so worried about making sure she's okay that even in his worst drug-infused benders, Candice was a top priority.

"No. I'm doing this for all selfish reasons. I don't want the world to think my wife is having an affair with that asshole." He rubs my back.

"Fair. How are we going to get back to our house?" I ask.

"Well, thank God we have a gate," he jokes. "I'll call Pete to pick us up here." Pete is our go-to security guard. While our day-to-day life is usually fine without security, we bring Pete whenever we have something like this happen or go out for the day with our daughter.

"It's probably surrounded now."

"Yup. Awesome."

"Guess we need to face the music."

"Yup," Knox says and his phone dings.

"What did he say?" I ask as Knox releases me.

"What a prick." Knox scowls. "He asked me who this was."

"Actually?" I stifle a laugh. "Mick may be a jerk, but that's pretty funny."

"I'm going to kill Candice and then Mick," Knox says through gritted teeth as he texts Mick back.

"Let's go easy on her. You can kill Mick, though." I smile.

"You're too easy on her all the time. You made me go easy on her in Spain last year when she was caught skinny dipping, and we had to bail her out of jail, or in Singapore when she went to buy rip-off designer bags and ended up getting robbed," Knox says.

"The rip-off designer bags was kinda hilarious seeing as how she could have gotten a real one." I giggle. Candice is always getting herself into some type of trouble—usually harmless trouble. Knox's phone dings again, and I can see the anger rise in his face.

"That motherfucker," he hisses and shows me the phone.

Mick: *Sure, sounds good. I'll pretend I wasn't banging your sister in your house.*

"Knox, I'm sure that's not true. Let's go home and talk to Candice," I say.

"Fine," he says, and he begins to type furiously again.

"What are you doing this time?" I ask and pick up the clothes we had thrown around the room. We should be having breakfast in bed, but this is our life now—stolen moments of privacy.

"Tweeting our 'story' so Mick can retweet it." He reads whatever he's concocted for a few more seconds before he shows it to me:

Great night catching up with @MickDTalons! Thanks to my wife for putting up with the stories! #greatnight

"Perfect." I hit the send button.

"I fucking hate him," Knox says.

"I know."

"I really, really want to punch him."

"So do I," I say. Knox's phone beeps.

"Mick retweeted it already and replied," Knox says, "so good to see you too @KBHestons and your beautiful family! #greatnight #allnighter." Knox lets out an audible breath.

"He had to hashtag all-nighter, huh?" I ask.

"Yup, of course, he did." Knox grabs his bag and my new guitar. "Let's go."

I grab my bag as well, then loop my arm around Knox's. His hands are too full to hold mine, but if I let him go, he might break out into a run and go to Mick's and hit him. The Claridge's has a private garage where Pete is waiting for us. We hop in the SUV. The drive back to our place is quick but silent. Paparazzi surround our house. Pete punches in the code and pulls into our driveway. Knox can barely contain himself as he bursts out of the car.

"Knox." I grab his hand. "Take a deep breath."

"I will," he replies as he opens our front door.

"Candice Eloise Bryan!" Knox's voice fills the alcove as he enters the front door. "Who was at our house last night?" Knox storms from the front door to the living room where she's sitting. I follow closely behind him, knowing this is already starting on the wrong foot. The only good thing is that Lottie is at her friend's place for a playdate I had arranged earlier in the week. She won't have to witness her father get mad at her favourite auntie.

"Uh—" she starts.

Knox cuts her off. "Just in case you were wondering, there are photos."

"Photos? Where?" Her eyes go wide.

"Paparazzi, Candice! You should know this by now. Mick was seen sneaking out of our house," Knox growls.

"It's not what you think," she says.

"See, I told you." I touch Knox's arm. At this moment, I'm the only reason he's going to stay sane at this moment. However, I doubt my powers right now.

"He stopped by when I told him I wasn't going to a rooftop party." Her eyes dart back and forth between us.

"You know what the worst part is? You have no idea what the tabloids are saying. Maybe Google him and see what comes up," Knox says.

Candice takes out her phone, and her face falls. "Oh. He was making out with some model last night."

"Are you okay?" Caroline asks.

"What? That's not what I meant," Knox says and grabs the phone out of her hands. "This is what I meant." He hands it back to her.

"Oh my gosh, Caroline. I am so sorry!" she says.

"Knox took care of it." I sit down beside her and squeeze her arm. There's something else going on here. Knox has no idea what's been going on with her—the Felix breakup has been extremely tough on her.

Knox shakes his head. "This can't happen again. I know Mick seems real charming, but he's an asshole, and you deserve better than him."

"We're not doing anything. I swear. We only talked, and then we fell asleep on the couch while watching a movie," she says.

"I believe you." Knox's tone softens. "But you've finally got a job you're excited about. Don't let anything jeopardize that."

"I won't—wait, did Rick see this?" She frowns.

"Who do you think told Caroline to check Google?" Knox says.

"Am I in trouble?" she asks, making eye contact with me.

"No. Only to try not to get into any more trouble..." I rub my face.

"Thank God."

"And another thing. How do you think Felix is going to feel? He knows you were watching Lottie last night," Knox says.

"Knox, I love you but get out now." I stand and put my arms around his shoulders to guide him to the stairs.

"What?" he frowns.

"Go upstairs or to the kitchen. I need to talk to Candice without you," I say. She doesn't need a lecture about Felix's feelings. Even though I love the guy, fuck him. He caused this breakup more than her.

"Caroline..." he starts, but I cut him off.

"No Caroline, anything. I say this with all of my love but go," I say as I place my hands on my hips. His brows furrow, but he does as he's told and leaves us alone.

"Are you okay, Candy?" I ask as I take a seat beside her again.

"Yeah. Why wouldn't I be?" She gives me a tight smile.

"Because of the first news story you read out."

"Oh, I don't care what he does."

"Candice." I grab one of her hands.

"Okay. I'm a little upset. We had a great chat. We played twenty questions, and he was actually honest—or so I thought."

"He can be—charming? I don't know. I've never seen that side of him, but with the number of girls who love him, I'm assuming it's true. But you have to remember he doesn't have the best reputation."

"I know. I'm so daft. I think I'm missing the security of a relationship. Going home to an empty house all the time—it feels depressing."

"I get it. I don't know what I'd do without Knox, so I can only imagine how you're feeling." Candice did love Felix, but I don't know if she was ever in love with him. Now without him, you could tell she's lonely. I'm so glad she moved to London. "Stay here again tonight. You don't need to go home. We have plenty of space."

"No, it's okay, Caroline. I can't do that." She shakes her head. I don't relent though.

"Yup, you are. You're going to go home, pack some clothes, and come back here. We're also going out tonight," I say.

"Is Knox going to be okay with it?" she eyes me carefully.

"I think so. He can watch Lottie, and I think he wanted to finish some songs with Felix anyway. Don't worry. I'll tell him to invite Felix over after we leave." I smile.

"All right, let's do it," she says.

"Awesome. I don't remember the last time I went out. You may have to help me pick out some clothes." Most of my wardrobe consists of leather jackets in different styles and ripped jeans in different colours.

"Can do! I'll bring you something from my closet."

"Nothing too slutty. Remember, I'm a mom." I laugh. "Where are we going to go?"

"Don't worry. I'll find something," she says. She stands and heads to the front door. She slides on her shoes and grabs her weekender.

"Okay, be back by three," I say. "Also, get Pete to drive you home. I know you like to walk, and it's not far, but with the number of paps outside, I'd feel better if our bodyguard is with you."

"Will do." She gives me one last nod before heading out the door.

"She's gone?" Knox comes down the stairs after the front door closes.

"Yup," I say.

"Good," Knox says.

"She's coming back, though. She's staying over tonight too, and we're going out."

"I don't want to go out tonight." He crosses his arms and leans against the wall.

"Good cause you're not invited. I feel bad that I haven't had time to go out with just her since she moved here, so tonight is a perfect time," I say.

"You are about to go on tour together. You'll find time to hang out," he says.

"Why are you so grumpy?"

"I'm not..."

"You are."

"Fine. I am. It's annoying. This whole situation is annoying me. Felix won't stop moping around, Candice is hanging out with a jerk, and you're busy all the time... I'm not used to it." He runs a hand through his hair. When Candice and Felix got together four years ago, Knox wanted it to be a quick fling he didn't have to hear about, but when it turned into something more, he was excited about the prospect of Felix being his actual brother. Without knowing the entire backstory of their breakup, he can't grasp the entirety of what happened.

"I know. It's an adjustment," I say. "Oh, if Felix is coming over tonight, can you ask him to come after 7?"

"Sure."

"I love you." I move closer to him and wrap my arms around him.

"I love you too." He squeezes me before he lets go.

"If you're awake when I get home tonight, we can totally do it."

"I'm holding you to that." He laughs.

"Good," I say. "Let's go hang out with our kid."

"I can't wear this." I groan from the closet. The green dress Candice has picked out for me is shorter and tighter than anything I've worn since getting into my 30s. Scratch that. It's shorter than probably anything I've ever worn period.

"Yes, you can," Candice calls back.

"I'm a mother, remember?" I ask.

"I'm well aware." She chuckles.

I come out of the closet, and she gasps.

"I'm changing," I say.

"No, you're wearing it. You look flippin' amazing." Candice smiles and starts to fuss over the dress, pulling it an inch higher, which I promptly pull back down.

"Of course, you'd say that. I look like you." I turn, looking in the mirror.

"Could be worse! Here put these on." She hands me sky-high black heels. Candice stands beside me and looks in the mirror. She's wearing a tight, royal blue tube dress that's a little shorter than mine, and her usually curly blonde hair is styled straight.

"What is the plan anyway?"

"Dinner then going to this sweet private party Nadine told me about," Candice says.

"Is Nadine going?" I try to hide my groan. Nadine hits on my husband every time she sees him despite her sleeping with Danny. She claims she didn't know we were married the first time it happened, but she hasn't really stopped doing it. Not only that but she's also left Candice high and dry a few times.

"She is. We should go, though! It's dinner time." She smiles, and it stops my protest.

We narrowly get out of the house alive. Felix came over earlier than expected, and I had to rescue Candice. I'll talk to Knox about that later. For now, I'm going to enjoy the night with my best friend.

I can only take the party we're at for another few minutes before I fall asleep standing up. Candice is saying goodbye when a deep voice comes from behind me.

"Can I get a ride with you guys? Rex is stuck at my house. Something going on with my pipes—" Mick says.

He's lying. He wants to spend time with Candice, and the way she's been looking at him all night, I know she wants to spend time with him too. "We aren't going home yet. We were going to stop by the diner near my house for some food—"

"Oh. No problem. I can walk or something. Hopefully, I don't get into another fight." He turns around.

"Fine." I sigh. "You can come with us. But listen to me and listen well; if you do anything to fuck anything up for Candice, I will kill you."

"Wow, mama bear is out." He holds his hands up.

"I'm very, very serious. Candice is my family, and I will have no issue slapping the shit out of you," I say.

"Chill, Miss Priss. I got the warning."

"Stop calling me that," she hisses.

"Everything okay here?" Candice's head swivels between us.

"Yup! Caroline invited me to come eat with you guys." He grins.

"I didn't exac—" I start.

"She wants to get to know me better. What a great tour manager." He winks at me.

I roll my eyes and cross my arms.

Candice hesitates. "Okay then."

We head down the elevator. As soon as the doors open, the flashes start.

"Shit. Now it's going to look like we're banging again," I mumble.

"Meh. You could do worse. Like your husband, for instance," Mick says. Candice shoots him a dirty look.

"I'm sure it'll be fine," Candice says to me.

When we get outside, I can hear photographers start to shout. We navigate through the stream of paps to where Pete is waiting in the black SUV.

"Mick! Are you and Caroline Harper-Bryan having an affair?" one shouts.

"Caroline do you and Knox have an open relationship?" another asks.

"Did you even think about your daughter?"

My stomach clenches. Whenever Lottie gets brought up in the press, I want to scream. She didn't ask for this. She shouldn't ever be brought up.

"We're not together," Mick says. I'm grateful he stepped in before I could retort something rude. That's the last thing we need.

"Mick, you've been spotted around the Bryan residence and now hanging out with Caroline. Are you sure nothing is going on?"

I sit in silence in the front seat of the SUV. I quickly text Knox we're heading to the diner.

Mick continues to talk to the reporters, "Very sure. Caroline is my tour manager and a great friend. I'm also good friends with Candice Bryan."

"Is Candice your new girlfriend?" A pap yells.

"Friends doesn't mean girlfriend. Thank you." He jumps into the car next to Candice, and the paparazzi keep yelling questions.

"You didn't have to do that," I say.

"A thank you would suffice."

I don't need to look at him to know that he's smirking.

"Thanks—I guess," I say.

We take off down the street. We get to the diner in record time and get settled into our booth. The girl at the front is so in love with Mick. She doesn't look really at Candice or me. Fine by me. The door chimes, and I look up to see my husband strolling towards us. He didn't tell me he was coming, but I'm so happy to see him as he slides into the booth next to me.

This night is about to get a whole lot more interesting.

10

KNOX

"Ladies, Mick." I nod at them. My eyes shoot daggers at Mick. The pictures of him sneaking out of my house still seared into my brain. I get it. He's a douchebag rock star. I wish he wasn't interested in being around my sister, though, or my wife. Not that he's a threat to me and my marriage, more an annoyance that keeps pissing my wife off.

"Uh, hey." Mick frowns. "Who's watching your kid?"

"Oh, she's old enough to be left on her own." I pick up a menu and smile at him.

"You're joking." His jaw drops. *What a fool.*

"Obviously," I say. "Pete went back to our house after he dropped you off. Plus, how could I miss a party?"

"The more the merrier," he says. We lock in an intense staring contest.

"Uhm. Wh-what can I uh get you uhm… all?" the server stammers. She looks at me, then Mick, then back to me.

"Burger, please," Caroline answers, but the tension between Mick and myself is palpable.

"Blueberry pancakes with whip cream, please." Candice orders.

"After you," I say to Mick.

"No, I insist you go first." He glares.

"I'll have a black coffee, and apple pie, please," I say but don't break our stare.

"I'll have the same thing as this one." He motions to Candice but still doesn't look away from me. "Oh, and a Stella."

The server takes her leave quick.

"Pancakes and beer. Classy." I huff.

"Having a beer isn't going to bother you, is it, mate? I know you have your vices."

"Nope. Beer wasn't really my thing."

"Okay, stop it right now, you two," Caroline says.

"Yes, come on. We're eating shitty food late at night. It should be enough to put our differences aside," Candice says.

"They're right." Mick smirks at me then puts an arm on the booth so he can slide closer to Candice.

"Fine," I say. If he moves another muscle towards her, I might combust.

We sit in another awkward silence.

"So," Caroline says. "How was Lottie tonight?"

"Good. She was all over Felix. It was difficult to get anything done," I say.

"How was Felix?" Candice asks, and Mick looks a bit wounded by the question.

"The way he's been for the last two months." I sigh.

"Is he sick or something?" Mick asks.

"No," I say. "Heartbroken is more like it."

My best friend spent the entire night in a daze after the girls left. Was it shitty to get him to come over earlier than expected so he'd for sure run into Candice? Maybe. But I want them back together. They both seem lost a bit without each other—or maybe it's just Felix.

"Knox—" Caroline warns.

"Dude's an arse." Mick shrugs.

The waitress places down four glasses of water, coffee for me and slides Mick his beer.

"You don't even know him," I say. What right does this douchebag have to talk shit about Felix? He's worse than him.

"If a guy cheated on my sister, I probably wouldn't be defending him," Mick takes a swig from his beer as the table goes silent.

My mouth goes dry instantly, and my heart is pounding in my ears. Felix cheated on Candice? But how could that be? I would have known that, wouldn't I? Sure, there were stories, but there always is in this business.

"What did you say? He cheated on you?" I look at Candice.

"Well—uh—" Candice seems to be at a loss for words.

"You told me those stories weren't true. He told me they weren't true. And I believed you both!" I look at Caroline. The anger is in full effect now. They both lied to me and so did Felix. I'll murder him. "Did you know about this?"

"I—I did." Caroline looks down at the menu.

"You didn't tell me? Neither of you thought to mention this to me?" I ask. They're rhetorical questions, but I need to know the reason I'm finding this out last and that Mick is the one who told me.

"Lower your voice!" Caroline whispers.

"What was I supposed to say? Hey, your guitarist and best friend cheated on me multiple times, so we broke up? Oh, and he thought a good way to keep me was to propose?" Candice's voice is hushed.

"You should have told me. Both of you should have told me. I'll fucking kill him." I go to get up, but Caroline pulls me back.

"Calm down," Caroline says.

"I can't talk to either of you right now." I stand up and head to the door.

Caroline is quickly on my heels, and Candice isn't too far behind.

My breathing is ragged as what feels like a panic attack sets in. *Remember to take deep breaths.* I can't see anything. I see only red. I pace up and down the sidewalk. The walk home is only ten minutes, but I don't head in that direction.

"Knox, I—" Caroline reaches for me, but I wrench away.

"Don't you dare. You lied to me, Caroline. You never lie to me." It's hard to swallow. She's the only person in this entire world I trust. She's the only person who tells me the truth about everything and now this.

"I couldn't tell you. It wasn't my secret to tell." She shivers.

"It's all my-my fault." Candice sniffs as tears spill down her cheeks.

She will not make me feel bad for her. They kept me in the dark about this. I'm the dipshit who listened to Felix talk his rubbish about not knowing why Candice broke up with him.

"You both should have told me." My heart rate starts to return to normal even though the anger is still pumping through my veins.

"I know." Caroline's voice is quiet.

"Knox, you can't take this out on Caroline. This is me. I was so embarrassed, and I didn't want to ruin The Hestons or your friendship with Felix. It all got out of hand." Candice shakes her head.

"You should know that you mean more to me than any band. Have I not proven that to both of you?" What do I have to do to show these two and my daughter that they come first—over everything?

"We know that, of course. We know how much you love the band and Felix." Caroline reaches for my hand, and I let her take it this time.

Everything fucked up in my entire life always comes back to the band. I love those guys and I love making music, but this shit isn't worth it. My family being hurt because they feel like they don't want to ruin this dream for me isn't right. It pushes me harder to consider what my options are outside of this world. Can we all go back to being regular people? I shake my head. It doesn't matter the reason why they didn't tell me. They kept this from me.

"I'm done with this tonight. I need a break—from both of you." My eyes meet Caroline's, and her face falls. I turn and walk down the street towards our place. Caroline's steps follow me, but she's a bit behind. Candice must have stayed behind. Good. She can fall in love with another prick for all I care.

Caroline goes to bed in our room, and I follow, only to grab my pillow.

"Knox come on," she says as she takes off her earrings.

"Not now." I head out of the bedroom and don't look back.

I head to our guestroom, realizing now there was no need even to bring my pillow. We have some here. Maybe it was the fact that it made Caroline feel bad. That's why I did it. I want her to feel as shitty as I do right now.

Lying on my back in the darkness, my mind races. This has all gotten out of hand. I close my eyes and hope that tomorrow, all of this will be something that we can figure out, but I know it's not going to be that easy.

Five days. Five long-ass days without talking or touching my wife, but I can't get over it. We've been able to keep things together in front of Lottie, but I've been spending most of my time at the studio. Felix and Danny have been out of town, which has been for the best. I don't know what I'd do if I saw Felix.

"Knox, you need to talk to Caroline." Roberto is sitting across from me at the studio. His dark hair is longer than I remember, and his hazel eyes stare back at me.

"She lied to me." I lean back in my chair and feel weightless for a moment before the pressure of my entire life comes crashing back down on my shoulders.

"Not about that. About these feelings, you're having. The other shit you'll work out because you're not going to let this argument be the end of you two. You're projecting. You don't want to deal with the real issue, so it's easier to lash out about something else."

"Christ, when did you get a psychiatrist designation?" I chuckle, and he playfully hits me on the arm.

"You know I'm right." He smirks.

I let out a breath. "Let's say you are. What do I do about it?"

"Admit it to more people than only me. Tell people you're struggling."

"I don't want to be the—face of this. I don't want people to pity me."

"Pity is better than bottling it up until you do something stupid."

"I'd be letting everyone down. Danny, my family, Felix too, even though I don't give a shit about him." I scowl.

"Right now. But you can't make Candice and Felix's problems yours. Sure, you can be pissed at him for hurting your sister, but you need to talk to him as well."

"Okay, thank you. You can go now before you annoy me even more." I look down at the soundbar, and he stands.

"Love you too, mate." He chuckles and squeezes my shoulder.

"Yeah, you too. Thanks again for everything. Even if I don't want to hear it right now."

"No problem. Call me any time." He gives me one last nod before heading outside.

I scribble some notes into my lyric book. A song about betrayal is suddenly so easy for me. But it's not about Caroline or Candice. It's about me. It's about all the crap I did to everyone else.

The door squeaks open behind me.

"Did you forget something fucker?" I chuckle and turn to see Felix standing in the doorframe. Every angry feeling comes rushing back, but I restrain myself.

"Hey stranger. You've been dodging me," Felix says as he takes a seat in the chair across from me.

"Yet here you are." I glare at him.

"What's going on? Did I do something?" His eyebrows scrunch together.

"I don't know. You tell me." I cross my arms and swivel in the chair to face him.

"I have no idea, Knox. If you're mad, we fucked off this week, you said you wanted space to work on things alone a couple of weeks ago."

"If that's what you think I'm upset about, then you're a fucking idiot. You cheated on Candice. How many times? How come she had to keep this secret from me, so I didn't kick the fucking shit out of you? You should have found the courage and told me your goddamn self." My veins are throbbing in my neck, but I stay seated.

Felix's naturally olive skin turns ghostly white. "She told you?"

"It doesn't matter how I found out. You're lucky I don't fucking kill you. That's my baby sister, and you fucking hurt her."

"I know." His voice is barely a whisper.

"That's it? Get out of here. I can't look at you. I'll see you when we get back on tour and not a second before. You and me? We're fucking done. You're lucky I don't replace your ass."

He nods but doesn't say anything as he stands. His steps fade down the hallway, and I hear the front door slam shut.

One confrontation down. Two more to go.

11

CAROLINE

The week is going by too quick. After Friday, I would be back on tour without my husband and my daughter. It isn't like Knox is talking to me anyways. Other than a few pleasantries and good nights before bed, we don't speak. It has to be the longest we've gone without any sort of affection since we met. Two days before we're set to leave, Candice is sitting in my office, having lunch with me. We haven't talked much either. Getting everything ready for the road has taken us in two different directions this past week.

"Knox still not talking to you?" She asks.

I hand her a sandwich I made this morning. We have been eating so much takeout at the rehearsal space that the bagged lunch is extremely welcome. "Nope. You?"

"No. I thought we were protecting him and The Hestons by not telling him. Now I feel like we made it even worse." Candice picks at the sandwich but doesn't take a bite.

"I know he hasn't said anything to Felix, and he's been going to the studio all week and hasn't come home with bloody knuckles or black eyes. Now to get him to talk to us..."

"We leave on Saturday. It's already Thursday." She places a palm on her forehead.

"I don't know what to do. We've never fought this before—even when he was doing coke," I say.

"I'm so sorry, Caroline. I shouldn't have told you."

"No, don't. It's good you did. You're my sister too, and I want to be there for you." I take a sip from the bottled water next to me. "Let's talk about something else. What happened after we left?"

We've been so busy I haven't even gotten the recap from her.

"Oh—" She pauses, and my eyes go wide.

"Please tell me you didn't sleep with Mick," I say as Candice avoids eye contact. "Candice. No. No no no."

"We didn't have sex if that's what you mean, but I did sleep there—in the same bed as him."

"On Saturday?"

"Yes."

"But you were in the house when I woke up."

"I got his bodyguard to drop me off before you woke up," she says.

I knew we needed to get Lottie a dog for things like this. "Nothing else happened though, right?"

"Well—not exactly."

"What does that mean?" I ask.

"We kissed, but it was like a thirty-second kiss. Nothing crazy. We didn't do anything else, I swear," she says.

"Damn, Candice." I shake my head. "So, what's going on now?"

"Nothing. I'm avoiding him," she says.

"Probably for the best. I've told you how much of a nightmare he's been this week." I take a bite of my sandwich.

This week at rehearsals, Mick has yelled at me a total of ten times for the most minuscule details. His meltdowns are adding to the list of anxieties that are creeping into my brain. If this is a reflection of the next ten months, then I'm screwed.

"Caroline?" Conner McDowell pokes his head into my office. Conner, a Scot, has spiky blonde hair and tattoos up his arms. Conner has to be my second favourite, next to Brandon. He's always a gem, even if he is a bit of a cheeky flirt.

"What's up?"

"Can I talk to you for a moment?" he asks.

"You bet." I nod.

Candice stands and grabs the uneaten sandwich to take with her.

"You look beautiful today, Candice." Conner grins at her.

"Never going to happen, Conner." She pats him on the shoulder, and I stifle a giggle.

"Sure, babe. That's what they all say."

"How can I help?" I ask him as he takes a seat.

"I was wonderin' if you could talk to the lads for me. Mick's saying that we need to rehearse late tonight, and I really want to go see my mum. We're leaving on Saturday, and I won't have a chance to see her before then." He scratches his neck. Rick had mentioned that Conner's mum is sick and has been for quite some time.

"Sure," I say. "I think that's a reasonable request. What time do you need to be gone by?"

"Six would be best."

"We've been working late every night this week, so it shouldn't be a problem."

"Thanks so much. I appreciate it." Conner smiles and leaves.

I sigh and stand up. This is going to be fun. First, I talk to Kane and Brandon, both of whom really want to leave to see their partners. Then I talk to Rick, who looks like he hasn't slept in days, and he also agrees. This is all going too easily. Now to find Mick and Tommy.

"Can I talk to you boys?" I ask Tommy and Mick, who are having a drink in Mick's dressing room.

"If you must." Mick takes a sip of his drink.

"I talked to the other guys, and they would really appreciate being done by six tonight. Seeing as how we have early rehearsals tomorrow for the show, I don't see an issue." I stand tall to feign my confidence. Mick has managed to cause me to doubt myself, something I'll never admit to him.

"Oh, you don't see an issue? So, when Conner keeps missing the chord change in 'Bad Things' or when Brandon can't seem to hit the high note in 'Gonna Get Ya' or when Kane misses his cue for 'My Amazing Girl', it's all okay because Miss Priss doesn't see an issue?" Mick is furious.

"Come on, mate. A night off wouldn't be the worst thing…." Tommy starts, and Mick glares at him.

"There are flaws with every show, but working until your eyes bleed isn't the cure." I cross my arms. "People need time to recuperate."

"Tell me which band you were in that was as popular as us? Scratch that, tell me any band that you were in that even played one show." Mick stands with his drink in hand.

"Whatever. If you want to stay here, that's fine, but I'm giving everyone else the night off. I spoke to Rick too, and he agreed." I shrug.

"You don't get to make that fucking choice."

"Have fun alone then." I turn my back and hear Mick throw a glass against the wall, causing me to flinch.

"Caroline, you don't get to choose what this band does and doesn't do!"

"I didn't make the choice. Everyone else asked for it!" I shout back.

The door beside me opens, and Brandon steps out into the hallway.

"You okay?" He asks me.

"Oh yeah. I'm dealing with Hurricane Mick. The poor glass was a casualty of his bad temper," I say.

"We've been here almost twelve hours a day since we started practicing for this tour. I told Hannah I'd help her pack." Brandon sighs.

"Yes, go home. I need to see my kid also before we take off. She's coming to work with me tomorrow and then to the show," I smile.

"Awesome!" Brandon says. "Thanks for talking to Mick."

"Not a problem. I prefer the explosive temper to the silent treatment. At least you know what's going on in their head." I frown.

"Problems at home?" Brandon asks.

"You could say, but it'll be all right," I say, and he gives me a sympathetic look. "All right, B, have a good night. Enjoy your time with your girlfriend. Let me know if things go south at rehearsal."

After another few hours of work, I fiddle with my pens as I know I need to talk to Mick once more before I leave. It's the mature, responsible thing to do, even though I'd rather eat rocks than suck up to that ass. I leave my office to search for him.

"See you tomorrow, Car." Conner whistles as he continues down the hallway.

"Yeah. See you," I say. *Glad he's happy.* I knock on the door of Mick's dressing room.

"What?" He shouts.

"Hey," I say as I open the door.

"You can leave." He's sitting on his couch.

"I wanted to talk to you before I left." I lean against the wall.

"How lovely."

"What's your problem with me? Honestly, spit it out. I think I've proven that I have some inkling as to what I'm doing, so why are you fighting me so much?"

"Because you've never had to work for anything in your life. You've had everything handed to you because your husband is famous." He shrugs.

"I met my husband when I worked as a guitar tech for Feline… the band who opened for The Hestons in the early 2000s," I say.

"You can play the guitar? Play me something." He hands me his acoustic guitar.

"Fine. Any requests?" I sit on the couch across from him.

"Why not 'My Amazing Girl'? Might as well stay in the family." He intertwines his fingers and places them behind his head.

I strum the first few notes. I memorized the chords to that song. Mick sits up a little straighter, and I can tell he wasn't expecting me to be able to play one note, let alone the entire song. When I finish, he's still looking at me.

"Huh. Well then, I guess you can play," he says.

"Are you going to be nice to me?" I place the guitar down.

"Naw. I don't think that would be much fun." He sits up straighter.

"Fine. At least be nice to Candice."

"Did she say I wasn't being nice?" he frowns.

"You know what is really shitty? Telling her brother that his best friend and her ex-boyfriend cheated on her," I narrow my eyes. Mick was the whole reason my marriage had been hell this last week.

"Look, I had no idea Knox didn't know. What a shitty friend and wife you are by not telling anyone or making Candice tell Knox herself."

Touché.

"I was trying to protect him and The Hestons," I say.

"At the expense of your supposed best friend. Yeah, makes sense to me," he scoffs.

"I did what I thought was best, and Candice begged me not to tell him because she always got back together with Felix. I honestly thought she was happy, and this is what she wanted."

Candice had put up a good front when she and Felix were together. No one knew they were unhappy, so why was I going to be the one to ruin that and create a divide? Still, Mick isn't wrong.

"Like I said, great friend." He stands and throws on his leather jacket.

"Well, if the papers are any indication, Candice would be better off being with Felix," I say as Mick tenses.

"Don't you ever say that." He turns to face me. He's close enough that I can see the veins in his neck straining—touchy subject.

"Oh, so you do like her? Funny way of showing it. Ignoring her all week is super Prince Charming of you. She's a good girl. Don't mess her life up," I say and stand as well.

"Why do you think I'm staying away from her?" he whispers.

"She cares about you, God only knows why, but she does. At least man up enough to talk to her. And for once in your life, be honest," I say.

"An honesty lecture from you. Really rich. Go on, Caroline. Enjoy your early night off," he says.

"I plan to," I open the door.

"Tell your husband I say hi… that is if he's talking to you." Mick slams the door behind me.

I drop Candice off at her place and tell her I'll be around early to pick her up. Now time to face the music.

"Hello?" I call as I get into my house.

"Hi mum." Lottie runs down the stairs and jumps into my arms.

"Hi beautiful. How was your day?" I ask.

"Good. Dad played me a song!" she replies.

"Did he now?" I ask.

"Yeah, and Felix let me play with his guitar." She smiles. I kiss her and place her on the ground.

"That's nice! Where is Dad?" I ask.

"He's in your room," she says.

"I'll be right back to make you some dinner," I say.

"Okay." She runs off to the living room.

As I start to climb the stairs to my bedroom, the anxiety in the pit of my stomach twists. The door is open, and I see Knox sitting on our bed, reading something in his journal.

"Hey," I say and walk into our room.

"Hey," he says but doesn't lookup. I sit down on the opposite side of the bed.

"How are you?" I ask.

"Good." He still doesn't look at me.

"Knox—"

"I'm busy, Caroline. Is this important?" he asks.

"You're busy, are you? Well, fuck you." I stand. "I've apologized to you for the past week. It wasn't my secret to tell, and your sister asked me not to tell you. Yes, you're my husband, but she's my friend, and I owe her some sort of confidentiality."

"Caroline..." His gaze meets mine.

"No. You're doing this to hurt me. I get it. Congrats Knox. You've made this past week unbearable. I can't wait to embark on a ten-month tour knowing that the last week I had with my husband was spent with us not even looking at each other." Tears sting my eyes as they fall down my cheeks.

"Hey, hey, now stop that." His voice is soft, and he stands up to move closer to me.

"Do you not want to be with me anymore? Is this the thing that sinks us?" I ask and look up at him. He wraps both arms around me.

"Don't you ever think that. I'm not going anywhere ever. Yes, I am fucking pissed at you, but I love you more than my right arm, so no, this isn't what sinks us. I can't believe neither of you told me. I would have never treated Candice the way that I have these past months. Jesus, I called her selfish…" He stops. I can hear him struggling not to choke up. "I put him over my own sister only for it to actually be all his fault."

"Knox, don't blame yourself for this. This is Candice and Felix's relationship. We can't be involved as much as we want to be." I sigh.

"He hurt her, Car. He hurt her so bad, and I-I." One of his tears hits my ear.

"Please don't cry," I say. I've only seen Knox cry a handful of times, and it kills me every time.

"I'm not crying." He lets go of me and rubs his eyes.

"Right," I smile.

"It sucks. I wish that she felt comfortable enough to tell me."

"I know, but you're her brother. She doesn't want you to know things like that—and it's Candice. She's a little more stubborn than most."

"True. Ah. I'm so mad. And you leave in two days, and I've been an arse."

"You have the rest of your life to hang out with me."

"I'm sorry," he says.

"I'm sorry too," I say, and he pulls me into him again.

"I love you."

"I love you too."

"Good. Now one more thing, and we are never talking about this again," he says and lets go of me. "Please don't lie to me again about something like that. That's big. I don't care who Candice sleeps with, but that was too big not to tell me."

"I will tell you if it happens again, but I hope it doesn't," I say.

"You and me both. Felix and I got into it."

"When?" I gasp. Knox and Felix have never argued in the entire time I've known them.

"Earlier. Roberto stopped by, and I thought it was him coming back, but it wasn't. He knew I was avoiding him. I snapped and told him he was dead to me."

I rub his back. This must be killing him. "I'm proud of you for standing up for Candice, but I wish it didn't come at the cost of your best friend."

"Same." He nods.

"Can you do me a favour?"

"Anything."

"Call your sister and tell her you love her. She missed you as much as I did this past week," I say.

"I'll call her," he says.

"Are you still coming to the show tomorrow?" I ask.

"Wouldn't miss it for anything, my love." He smiles and kisses me.

"God, I've missed you," I say.

"Me too. Let's never do this again," he says.

"Never."

And for the first time in a week, my world is right again.

12

KNOX

Everything Caroline has been working on these past few weeks boils down to the tour kick-off concert in London tonight, the night before they take their tour to the United States. I'm so happy for her. Lottie is buzzing in the seat next to me. I swear this kid is definitely a good mix of both of us. She loves live shows as much as we do. She's also been talking about Mick non-stop since his impromptu sleep-over at our place. Lottie's hand is intertwined with mine as we walk down the hallway toward Caroline's office.

"Mum!" Lottie screams.

"Hi, baby." She jumps onto Caroline's lap.

"Whoa, is this my wife?" I ask. Caroline's makeup is fully done. I'm guessing Candice had something to do with that.

"Still me." She smiles at me and places Lottie on the ground. She gets out of her chair and walks towards me.

"Hi." I pull her close and kiss her.

"Carol—oh, sorry." Mick steps inside. "Didn't mean to interrupt a little afternoon..."

"Mick!" My daughter shouts.

"Hello," he says and gives her a nod. She runs over to Mick and wraps her arms around his legs. Mick looks uncomfortable.

"Lottie, that's enough. Let Mick go." Caroline suppresses a laugh.

"Sorry." She blushes and walks back over to us.

"It's fine, darling." He winks at her, and she giggles. *Oh brother.*

"Stop trying to charm my five-year-old," I say.

"Like all Bryan girls, they find me irresistible." He smirks.

"Hardly." Caroline laughs.

"You're not a true Bryan now, are ya?" Mick says. "Anyways, I need to know if you arranged for my guitars to be packed up in the front of the van?"

"Yup. Front and centre," she says.

"Good. Thanks," he says.

My eye is drawn to his bloody knuckles. "What happened to your hands?"

"Ask your mate Felix."

"You didn't—" My jaw drops. Maybe I do like Mick after all.

"I'll tell you about it after," Caroline says to me. "You should go pack, and Knox you should probably get back to the studio if you're going to make it back for the concert."

"Yes ma'am," I say.

"What about me?" Lottie pouts.

"Come on kid. You can help me pack," Mick says. Caroline and I exchange looks.

"Yay. Can I mummy?" she asks.

Caroline hesitates. There's a palpable silence hanging over us all.

"I used to watch my sister all the time." Mick shrugs. Caroline looks at me.

"Sure," Knox says. "Be good."

"I will, Dad," Lottie says.

"No swearing," Caroline says to Mick as he shuffles Lottie out of the room.

"No promises."

"You said yes?" she asks when it's the two of us.

"Why not? What's the worst that could happen? You're down the hall," I say.

"Are you feeling okay?" she teases me.

"Well, with Lottie being gone, it gives us a few minutes…" I lock her office door.

"Knox Leonardo Bryan," she says.

"Leonardo?" I laugh.

"You don't have a middle name, so I wanted you to feel normal like the rest of us." She giggles, and I wrap my arms around her waist.

"I'm going to miss you." I kiss her forehead.

"Me too." She kisses my lips lightly.

"So, three weeks from now, you have a break?" I ask.

"Yup," she says. "Four whole days. I already booked a ticket to Paris to meet you guys."

"Awesome. I'm so going to…" I start.

"We have fifteen minutes. Do you really want to keep talking?" She raises her eyebrows.

"No ma'am." I kiss her again.

"Good." She giggles, and I hoist her onto her desk.

I trail kisses from her lips to her neck as my hands massage her breasts through her shirt. "On second thought—"

I pull her onto her feet and turn her around, so her palms are on her desk.

"Mr. Bryan, Do we have a bit of a fuck me on the desk fetish?" She asks.

"I think everyone man has a fuck Caroline on their desk fetish." I smirk as my hands run from her back to her ass. I give her a quick slap before wrapping my hands around the front of her jeans and unbutton them. I tug them down her thighs and notice she's wearing a red thong.

"Christ, woman. Are you tryin' to kill me?" I grind my erection against her ass. Even with pants on, she can feel how hard she makes me.

"Oh," she breathes out.

I slide off her panties, and she steps out of them. I pull her shirt over her head quickly before turning her back towards the desk. I undress so fast I almost fall over.

I rub against her wet core. This time there are no barriers between us. The tip of my cock teases her folds before I push into her.

Caroline lets out a low moan as she tightens around my dick. "Oh God, Knox."

I let out a growl at the sound of my name. I thrust into her hard, and she starts to pant as my hips increase their speed. We don't have time to waste, with only a few minutes stolen before people will come looking for us.

"Keep doing that. You feel so good," Caroline says. I pump harder, and she grips the desk tighter.

"Come with me," I say.

Caroline's breathing gets harder, and I can tell she's about to fall off the edge. My thrusts increase. I'm hitting the right spot because Caroline tenses around me and pulsates. She bites her knuckle to keep from screaming. I let out a low moan as I explode into her. I pound out every last wave of my release, jerking to a stop. I slowly pull out of her, and wipe sweat from my brow. Caroline stands up and turns to face me.

"Great job being quick and efficient, babe." She smiles then leans in to kiss me.

"We had a time limit I didn't intend to break." I wink at her as I pull my underwear and pants back up. Caroline gets dressed, and it pains me to see her fully clothed again.

"Duty calls," she says and gives me one last kiss. "Thanks for the sex."

"I will make office calls any time for you, babe," I say.

I give her one last kiss and then say our goodbyes. Only a few more hours till I can hopefully repeat this matinee.

After finishing up at the studio, I make it to the second half of the concert. I end up standing with Rick on one side of the stage. We're chatting back and forth with Mick's voice in the background.

"How's everybody doing tonight?" Mick says to the crowd, and they scream. "Wonderful! This next song you might all know off our newest album. I have to say it's my favourite. This one goes out to our newest employee, Candice Bryan."

My entire body tenses as he begins to play.

"That's going to be trouble." Rick chuckles and shakes his head.

"You're not mad?" I ask.

"If I've learned anything in this business, it's that you can't keep two people who are meant to be away from each other."

Meant to be? "I don't think they're meant to be."

"She looks at him like Caroline looks at you and vice versa. You know as well as I do that there's no point in getting in the way. As long as the tour goes ahead, and nothing fucks that up, then I'm happy." Rick slaps me on the back and leaves me.

He can't be seriously thinking that these two are going to work out. Mick is worse than Felix. Candice needs to be with someone who treats her like a queen.

The show ends, and I speed walk to the other side of the stage. As soon as I get there, Mick has Candice in a hug, and they're laughing. She hasn't laughed like that in ages. Her smile as their eyes meet isn't one I've seen before. *Could Rick be right?*

"Isn't this cute." I interrupt their moment. Candice pushes Mick away.

"We were messing around." Candice shrugs.

"You guys are like kids," I say.

"Sorry, grandpa." Mick crosses his arms.

"Where's my wife?" I ask Candice.

"Over there." She points to Caroline, who's laughing with Brandon and Lottie. I don't move.

"I'm gonna go shower. See you later ya?" Mick says to Candice.

"Yep," she says as she looks at the ground. Mick gives me a nod before he disappears.

"What's going on with you two?" I quiz her.

"Nothing. We're friends." She shrugs.

"Similar to when you were 'just' friends with Felix? Don't do this to yourself again. You deserve better than this life." I sigh.

"You realize how hypocritical that sounds, right?" She scoffs.

"I know. But look at all the shit I put Caroline through. Look at all the shit Felix did. And Mick, well, he's younger than us and better looking." I joke to ease the tension. I'm not trying to hurt her; I'm trying to protect her.

"You're right." She hesitates. "I must have been caught up in the moment."

"We all get caught up in things. I love you, Candy. I'm your big brother, and I wasn't there for you when it came to Felix, but I'm always here."

I reach out and hug her. She squeezes me.

"Dad!" Lottie says from behind us.

"Hi, baby girl." I let go of Candice and grab Lottie as she runs towards me. She's wearing pink noise-cancelling headphones, and she tosses them to the side as I grab her.

"Hey! Don't throw your stuff." Caroline laughs as she joins us.

"Think about what I said ya?"

"I will." She nods before taking off towards the dressing rooms.

"What was that about?" Caroline asks.

"Oh, a bit of friendly brotherly advice." I smile, and Caroline's eyes narrow.

"Uh-huh. Let's go home before you offer anyone else 'brotherly' advice." She holds a hand out to me, and we intertwine our fingers before Lottie grabs her other hand.

When we get home, Lottie is immediately put to bed. Not only because it's way, way past her bedtime, but I want uninterrupted time with Caroline. I kiss my daughter good night quickly and head into our bedroom. Caroline is pacing around, throwing last-minute things into her suitcase. I take a seat on the edge of our bed.

"Do I need this?" She holds out earplugs.

"They're never a bad thing to have. You are also sharing a room with Candice, and if I remember correctly when we were kids, she was an epic snorer." I smirk.

"Oh, so that runs in the family." She winks.

"Ouch." I chuckle. She continues to wander around the room. "Please come sit with me. You've packed one hundred times already. As long as you have your passport and wallet, everything else can be replaced."

She stops and grabs my outstretched hands. She stands between my legs and places her hands on each of my shoulders. "I know. I'm a bit anxious, if I'm being honest."

"Not surprising. It's all brand new again." I tug her to sit beside me, and

I place my arm around her shoulders. She wraps her arms around my waist and snuggles in tight.

"I wish you were coming," she whispers.

"Let's not waste time trying to change what's going to happen tomorrow. Kiss me, baby, and everything is going to be all right." I lean in, and she meets my lips.

I'm going to soak up every last second with her.

"Call me when you get there," I say as I hug Caroline for the third time in two minutes. Lottie is hugging both of our legs.

"I will," she says. She's fighting to hold back tears.

"Pete, can you come grab Lottie?" I ask. Pete strolls over as Caroline bends down to talk to Lottie one more time.

"Be a good girl. I'll Skype you every chance I get, all right?" She hugs her tightly.

"Okay, mum. I love you," she says.

I'm starting to hope that kids are like dogs, and they don't really grasp the concept of time. Because if Lottie knew that this is the last time she's going to see her mum for three weeks, she'd probably be a bit more hysterical.

"I love you too." Caroline gives her one last hug before Pete picks her up to take her to the car. As soon as she's out of sight, Caroline begins to cry.

"Hey, shhh. None of that." I pull her into my chest. I stroke her hair, hoping it's soothing.

"I'm sorry." She sniffs and wipes at her eyes. "I want to go, but I don't at the same time. You probably think I'm crazy."

"Crazy Caroline does have a ring to it." I tease. "Baby girl, you have got to get on that plane. Trust yourself that you made the right decision."

"It's going to be weird not driving home at night and you texting me something stupid like 'pick up ice cream' and getting into bed with you instead of alone." She's rambling. Caroline rambles when she's nervous.

"Caroline…" I grab both of her hands. "We can do that again in ten months. Hell, I can text it to you when you're visiting us in Paris. Don't act like this is forever."

"You're right." She sighs. "I love you."

The selfish part of me wants her never to leave my arms, but I know this is right for her. Even if she is my sense of security, they taught us in rehab to be able to rely on ourselves and our own strength to get through the hard times, but unintentionally Caroline has become the source of my strength.

"I love you too. So so so much, my darling." I kiss her left hand then right.

"Be good. Take care of our daughter. Call me every night and text me every day," she says.

"Yes, ma'am. I love you," I say again and kiss her—not wanting ever to stop.

"I love you too," she says.

"Caroline?" Rick calls from behind us.

"Coming." She grabs her bag and turns back to me. "Bye."

"See you soon," I say.

With one final kiss, she turns around and walks away. Thankfully, she doesn't turn back because I don't think my resolve would hold if she did. I'd run to her, throw her over my shoulder and take her back home with us. She fades out of my view, and I take that as my cue to go.

Everything is going to be fine.

13

CAROLINE

Candice loops an arm in mine as I slide my sunglasses down to hide my tears. "I know it's hard, but we're going to have so much fun."

"I know you're right, but shit, does this suck." I sniff.

"At least we have each other," she smiles.

"Yeah, at least we have each other," I reply. We head out onto the tarmac, and Candice starts to laugh.

"What's so funny?" I ask.

"Us on private planes. Do you remember the first time I met you?" she asks.

"How could I forget?" I ask. The first time I met Candice, she was fifteen, and I was twenty-one. Knox and I had been together for about two years, but because of a crazy tour schedule and us spending most of our off time sleeping or having sex, it took me that long to meet his family.

"God, I was trouble back then." Candice interrupts my memory.

"Back then? How about you're trouble, period." I laugh. Candice managed to convince me to go out that first night, even though technically, she was too young to be clubbing. We had gotten so incredibly drunk that the hangover the next day was unbearable. We were both puking. Knox was pissed.

"Caroline, can I talk to you for a quick sec?" Mick stops us. Candice looks at me, then Mick.

"I'll just go talk to Brandon." She excuses herself.

"What can I do for you?" I ask. My eyes narrow, unsure of what his request could possibly be.

"You're flying with me in my plane today," he says.

"Is that a question or a demand?" I ask.

"Both?"

"You hate me, so why do you want to share a tiny space with me for the next eight hours?"

"I just do." He glances over at Candice.

"Candice thinks I'm on your plane, and if I'm not, then she'll follow me, and you can't watch her every move." I raise my eyebrows at him. Man, this kid has it bad for her.

"I don't need to watch her." He scoffs.

"Don't you, though?" I smirk and look back at Candice, who's now talking to Conner. Mick's face is turning red. "I don't want you to have a heart attack because my paycheck relies on you being alive, so I'll do it under one condition. If you're rude to me even once, then I'll never do you another favour."

"Deal." He grits his teeth.

"Sheesh, you've got it bad." I shake my head and walk to Candice. She smiles at me as I get to her and Conner. Conner turns to chat with Kane and his wife, Charity.

"Can we sit together?" Candice asks.

"You don't want to sit with Mick?" I ask.

"No, I don't. I have to tell you something, but I don't want to tell you because you're going to freak out and..." She babbles as we walk on the tarmac.

"Candice, tell me because we know you're going to." I laugh. She grabs my arm before I can step on the first stair to board the plane.

"I slept with Mick last night—well, technically three hours ago," she says.

"What! You didn't!" I gasp.

"I did."

I pause.

"Caroline, say something."

"Was it good?"

Candice had already slept with him. What was the point in treating her like a child?

"So good. Ugh. Amazing. But what do I really have it to compare to? Felix was it," she says.

"Was he better than Felix?" I ask.

"Way better." She sighs.

"So, what's going on now?" I ask.

"Nothing. Nothing at all, actually. We have a deal that we aren't going to be with anyone else for ten months," she says.

"As your friend, I'm going to tell you that's a terrible idea. You got out of something, and now you're saving yourself for someone with who you aren't supposed to have a relationship with. Plus, good luck surviving ten months if he's the best you ever had," I say.

"I know. It's dumb. It's super dumb..." she says.

"But?"

"But I don't know. I've never felt this twisted up about something."

"Do you love him?"

She avoids eye contact. "I..."

"Ladies, we must be going," Rick calls to us.

"Sorry!" I say.

"No problem. Get up here!" He motions for us to follow him.

"We're not done with this conversation," I whisper to her.

"I know," she says.

When we get on the plane, there are two open seats across the aisle from each other. It just so happened that one is by Mick, and one is by Tommy. Candice immediately sits down by Tommy.

"What are you doing?" I hiss.

"I-I'm sorry. I can't," she whispers back. I let out a long sigh.

"You drew the short straw, I guess," Mick says to me as I take a seat.

"You guessed right." I rustle through my purse, looking for my phone. "I'm going to put on my headphones and pretend you don't exist."

"Good idea," I reply and slide on my own headphones. I almost start to cry as Knox's voice comes through the speakers. I slide my sunglasses down and lose myself in the music. It only takes a few minutes till I'm out cold.

"Caroline?" Mick's voice interrupts my nap.

"What?" I don't open my eyes.

"Switch me seats."

"No." I turn towards the aisle.

"Please," he says.

"Why?" I open my eyes and face him.

"I don't like this seat anymore," he says, and I glance at my watch. We've only been in the air for two hours.

"Fine." I sigh and stand up.

"Thanks," he says.

I sit down in my new seat. Candice is dead asleep next to Tommy. Mick sits down and stares at her.

"You're see-through, you know," I say to him.

"Oh, am I? How so?" He keeps his voice low not to wake Candice.

"You are so in love with her." I chuckle and grab a magazine.

"I've known her two weeks. How can you be in love with someone that fast?" He frowns.

"I'm not sure, but it happens," I reply.

"Seeing as how you're an expert and everything, how long did it take you to fall in love with Knox?" His tone is condescending, but I don't care. If this helps him realize his own feelings and it benefits Candice, then that's a win for me.

"I would say about ten seconds."

"You're joking."

"No. I mean, it took me a long time to admit it, but I knew the second I met him that he was going to be special to me," I say and think about the day I met Knox. I had been able to convince the tour manager for Feline to give me a chance as a guitar tech. When Knox walked into the room, I almost dropped the guitar I was working on. I had never seen someone so pretty and someone with such a presence about them.

"Bullshit." Mick startles me from my memory.

"Well, I guess it would be hard for someone like you to understand." I shrug.

"Someone like me?"

"Yeah, someone with no soul."

"Good one."

"She told me, you know."

"I knew she would," he says and glances back to a sleeping Candice.

"So, what are you going to do?" I ask.

"What do you mean?"

"What are you two now? Are you dating?"

"No. We're not dating." He shifts uncomfortably.

"Probably for the best." I nod.

"Oh? You don't think I'm right for her?" he asks.

"No, I don't." I shake my head.

"I care about her… even if you don't believe me," he says. Even though he's being genuine, I don't know if he knows what love is. Real love anyways.

"That's not the reason I don't think you're right for her. I don't think you're ready for what Candice would be for you," I say.

"What will she be for me?" Mick asks.

"She would be the girl who would turn your whole world upside down and love you completely—but that's not something you're ready for," I say.

He doesn't say anything, so I turn away.

I'm about to slide my headphones back on, and I swear I hear him mutter, "I'm ready."

Oh boy, this is going to be one interesting tour.

I wake up and look down at my watch. One more hour till we land. Candice is awake now and playing with her phone.

"Mick can you switch me seats?" she asks.

"Uh, sure." He gets up.

"Yeah, I'm definitely using you if I need him to do anything." I chuckle.

"Sorry about earlier," she says.

"For making me sit next to someone who hates me for eight hours? No problem." I smile.

"I owe you," she says. "Can I have some gum?"

"Yeah, for sure." I grab my bag and dig around. My hand wraps around something unfamiliar, and I pull out a piece of paper.

Caroline,
I love you and am so proud of you. Paris will be ours, and I cannot wait to hold you.
All my love always,
K

My heart squeezes, and Candice asks me what's up, but I shake my head. This is only for Knox and me.

We land in New York, and ease seeps into my bones. It's nice being back in North America. Not that I don't love London, but this is my side of the world. We grab our bags, and the team drives us through the streets of New York. Except driving might be a bit of stretch. It feels like we're in constant traffic and only move an inch every other minute. Finally, we make it to our hotel in Manhattan. Rick, Candice, and I check in together.

"Band meeting in room 2607 in an hour, okay?" Rick says to me.

"Sounds good. Is that your room?" I ask.

"Yup. Where are you two ladies?" he says.

"2504," I say.

"The boys are all on the twenty-seventh floor." Rick writes down our room number on a piece of paper.

"Sounds good. So do we have all three floors?" I ask.

"Yes. We spread the crew out, so everyone got their own room—except you guys. Crazy girls." He grins.

"I'm used to a hotel room with my kid and my husband, so having another person around will be comforting," I say.

"I'm used to a loud guitarist, so I also like having another person around." Candice smiles.

"You can sleep in my room then, doll." Conner comes up behind us.

"I'll pass, thanks. Caroline's a much better roommate, I'm sure," Candice says.

"Okay, how about I crash with you lasses?" he says.

"That'll be the day." I roll my eyes.

"Hopefully soon." Conner smirks and heads to the elevator.

"That boy." Rick shakes his head.

"So, how much trouble are we in for during this tour?" I ask.

"Probably a lot," Rick says.

"Might as well keep things interesting." I laugh.

"True! I'll see you in a bit." He nods and heads off.

Candice is staring at something. I look past her and see Mick laughing with the receptionist.

"Come on. Don't do this," I say to her.

"Do what?" she asks.

"Be the jealous girlfriend who's not a girlfriend."

"You're right." She shakes her head. "Let's get out of here."

"Hello, Caroline." Charlie smiles at me as he picks up his bags behind us.

"I thought I saw you earlier." I hug him.

"Yeah. I got hired last week. Hey Candice." He grins.

Oh no. If there's one thing that will cause more drama, it's Charlie being interested in Candice.

"Hi again," she says.

"If you guys don't have any plans later, I can show you around," Charlie says.

"I have a meeting, but I think Candice is free," I say.

"I uh." She looks at me then back to him. "Yeah. Sure."

"Great. I'll text you later." He gives us a wave before he takes off to catch up with another crew member.

"What the hell?" Candice says.

"What?"

"You know what. Mick is going to flip out."

Mick's still talking to the receptionist, completely oblivious to anything else. If he's trying to hurt Candice's feelings, it's working.

"Who cares? Tell him, and I'm sure there won't be any trouble. Plus, he'll be with me at the meeting," I say.

My first big meeting. This was the first time that I have to really lay down the law. Rick said he's going to ensure we get everything out in the open at this meeting too. My stomach clenches, thinking about Mick talking about Candice. After dropping my stuff off in the room and saying goodbye to Candice, I head to Rick's room.

"You can do this, Caroline. You've dealt with harder things." I take a deep breath before knocking on the door.

"Caroline!" He greets me as he opens the door.

"Hi, hi. Is it only us?" I ask as I enter the suite.

"Just us so far," Rick says and motions for me to follow him to the living room.

"Wow, this is beautiful," I say and take a seat on the couch. "Ready to kick this all off? I can't believe it's really happening."

"I am ready for this to start. I feel like there's been so much build-up and now having a full staff, I'm ready for everything to run smoothly." He sits beside me.

"No pressure, right?" I laugh.

"You're the best. I was right to hire you."

"The best? Hardly."

"Well, you've managed to do the job all while dealing with five creatively different, moody young boys." He chuckles, and I join him.

"I feel like they are worse behaved than my own daughter."

"Boys with too much money." He shakes his head.

There's a knock at the door, and Rick goes to answer it. He comes back to the living room with Brandon in tow.

"Good idea leaving the stopper in the door, so I don't have to get up all the time to answer it," Rick says as he sits back down beside me again.

"Hey Caroline," Brandon says.

"Hey, how are you?" I stand up to give him a quick hug.

"Good. The flight was decent. Hannah and I slept the whole way. How was your flight?" he asks.

"I got to sit by Mick so as good as can be expected."

"Don't lie, Caroline. It blew your mind," Mick says as he enters the living room with Tommy behind him.

"I doubt you know how to blow anyone's mind," I say. Panic shoots through my stomach. What if he makes a comment about Candice in front of everyone? Mick sits down across from me.

"Well, I've had nothing but rave reviews." He smirks, and I roll my eyes.

Conner comes in next bitching about how his room isn't a south-facing room and that the room service here sucks. Kane is last and doesn't say a word as he sits down beside Brandon.

"Shall we get started?" I ask.

"We want to get everything out in the open. This hasn't been the easiest time for everyone. Let's get all of our grievances out there." Rick stands and looks at them all.

"Shoot. We're open books." Brandon smiles.

"Speak for yourself," Mick mutters.

"What was that, mate?" Brandon glares at him.

"You're an open book because you've really got nothing going on." Mick shrugs.

"Well, not all of us can lead the exciting life you lead. How is our hair-stylist?" Brandon shoots back.

"Brandon!" I say. *Shit.*

"Sorry," he says.

"Say anything about her again, and I'll break your face," Mick says.

"Both of you, stop it," I say, and they go silent.

"If you want it out in the open, then here it is. I'm not really a fan of anyone in this room," Mick says.

"What?" Tommy looks crushed.

"Except for you." Mick corrects himself.

"Oh my gosh, for a second, I thought you guys broke up." Conner chuckles.

"Shut up." Tommy shoots daggers at him.

"Relax," I say. Keeping the peace is more a part of the job than I thought.

"I'm fine with everyone, I think." Kane shrugs, and nobody disagrees. Kane might be the only person in the band who has no drama. He didn't need extra attention; he didn't fight with anyone, and he was happily married. He is a tour manager's wet dream.

"What's going on with you and Candice?" Rick asks, and my mouth goes dry.

"Nothing," he says.

"Bullshit," Conner says.

"Nothing is going on there. We're friends, kind of." Mick shrugs. "We've hung out a few times, but that's it. She's not really my type."

Even though a part of me knows he's trying to protect her job, my blood boils as he says that. He avoids eye contact with me.

"She's definitely my type," Conner interjects.

"Shut up," Mick says.

"Let me know if anything changes," Rick says.

"While you're still incredibly popular, your brand could use a little work to keep everything moving in a positive direction," Rick says.

"Which means what exactly?" Brandon asks.

"Keeping all of your shit together and if people are watching, be nice," Rick says.

After two hours of going over the schedule, confirming the setlist for what felt like the millionth time, and getting each of their must-haves for their dressing rooms confirmed, it was finally free time. I was exhausted and hungry.

"Are you going to meet up with Candice now?" Rick looks at his watch. Mick slows his steps as not to look like he's eavesdropping.

"Uh no, actually she went out with Charlie," I say. Mick stands straight up.

"The guitar tech?" Rick asks.

"Yeah. He used to work on The Hestons tour. They're old friends," I reply.

"That's nice." He smiles.

I give him a wave before I head out into the hallway. Mick is standing close to the door.

"She's out with that prick?" he asks.

"Mick, this is going to be a long tour if you two don't sort this out. So, for all our sakes, please tell her you like her." I turn before he can reply.

I'm ready for a long bath and a drink.

14

KNOX

I'm a teenager again. Waiting by my phone all hours of the day for the girl I love to contact me. Thankfully cellphones have been invented since I was a teenager, so it can at least come with me everywhere I go. *Fuck I miss my wife.* Another day at the studio, but we leave soon for Copenhagen. I'm ready to get out of England so that I can be distracted from Caroline being across the Atlantic.

"Knox?" Felix says, and I turn towards him. It's the first time I've seen him since Mick and him got into a scrap. Caroline gave me the Coles' Notes version, and it's hard to say it didn't make me a little happy. Felix's nose is in a splint. Damn, Mick can really throw a punch.

"What happened to your face?" I ask, not letting on that I know.

"Fell down some stairs." He avoids eye contact.

Lie. What else has he lied to me about over the years? Best friend, my arse.

"Right." I nod and turn back to my lyric journal.

"I want to check that we're good?" He leans against the doorframe.

"Tricky question Felix," I say and face him once more. Confusion spreads over his features. "Are we good as band members? Absolutely. Will we ever be friends again? No. You are a lying sack of shit. You made my sister feel like she couldn't tell me about what you did. I'm not sure why she stayed with you so long, but I'm glad that's done now."

The anger pulses through my body.

"I've apologized to her—many times. And I'm sorry to you as well. You are my best friend, Knox. I get you hate me. Fuck I hate me. But I'll fix this shit." Felix lets out a breath.

"Doubtful. You can leave now. See you in Copenhagen."

"You're not practicing with us?" He asks.

"No. It's the same fucking songs we've been playing for almost twenty years. I think we can handle the set." I spin around in my chair and click through my phone.

Felix pauses.

The silence hangs thick between us, but I refuse to acknowledge he's still there.

"I am sorry. For everything." He sighs.

"Sorry—" a female voice I don't know says.

"No, come in," I say. Lena's text from earlier pops into my mind. "You must be Natalie."

"Yes!" She flashes me a wide smile. She can't be older than twenty. Her teeth sparkle against tanned skin, and her hair is dyed a dark auburn. Any man would find this woman attractive, which is why Felix is checking her out.

"This is Felix, and he's leaving now." I gesture for her to sit in the seat next to mine but don't look at Felix again. He turns on his heel and walks out of the room.

"I feel like I disturbed something." She bites her bottom lip.

"No, you're good. Thanks for coming so quick. I know leaving tomorrow doesn't give us much time to get to know each other, but Lena recommended you, and I called the other two families you've worked for. If you're interested, the job is yours." I smile at her.

"Really?" She asks.

"Yeah. You're saving my life, honestly, so hopefully that's you saying yes."

"Yes! I would love to. Honestly, it'll be so cool to see the world." Natalie brushes a piece of hair out of her face. She looks even younger than she did when she walked in.

"Promise me one thing," I say.

"Sure!" She says.

"Don't let Felix or Danny take you out. They're known to be players." I shake my head.

"Good thing they're not my type. You are actually." She chuckles.

"Oh—" I shift awkwardly in my seat.

"Ohmigod. I didn't mean that—the way that sounded. I'm so sorry. Wow, way to go, Nat." She berates herself.

"It's all right. No problem." I laugh. "I'm sure I've said things similar."

"Thanks, Mr. Bryan. I'll get all the details from Lena." She grabs her purse, and we both stand. I tower over her. She can't be more than 5'3.

"No problem. I look forward to working together. I'm sure Lottie will love you." I offer my hand to her to shake.

She takes it. "Sounds great."

With one last wave, she leaves, and my bad mood from earlier is back. Everything about this tour is already fucked, and I don't even want to go. If everyone wasn't relying on me, I'd quit. But I can't. I'm stuck.

Copenhagen is as beautiful as always. With the colourful houses along the Nyhavn embankment, it's breathtaking. My dream would be to buy a place here for family trips. There was a time when Caroline and I would talk about having more kids, but that doesn't look like it will happen now. I wouldn't mind another daughter, but it would be incredible to have a son. One of each. The perfect family. But the thoughts of a son always come with the worry that he'd be like me. He'd suffer from the same vices as me. I don't have to worry about Lottie because she's as intelligent as Caroline. What if our son doesn't end up so lucky?

"Dad!" Lottie calls to me from the SUV. I had gotten so lost looking at the river that everything else had melted away momentarily.

"Let's go find our room, shall we?" I smile at her as Natalie grabs her other hand. We walk into the hotel, and I grab the keys to my room and give Natalie the key to hers. There's no way we're sharing a room, even though mine is a suite with multiple bedrooms.

"See you back here in a few hours so you can grab Lottie before I head to soundcheck," I say to Natalie. "You guys can come to the show tonight, so I'll arrange a car to come pick you guys up.

"Yes!" Lottie cheers. That girl loves the stage.

"Sounds great, Mr. Bryan." Natalie nods before heading into the elevator.

"Hi, Uncle Felix!" Lottie waves at him. Felix and Danny had travelled to Copenhagen yesterday, probably so they could party.

"Hi darlin'," Felix says. Lottie wraps her arms around his legs, and he bends down to scoop her up into his arms.

I may hate him right now, but my daughter loves him, and he's always been good to her.

"How was the trip?" Felix asks her.

Lottie babbles on about what movie she watched on the flight over. I get distracted by my phone. Caroline has texted a few times, but I haven't responded. Since this morning, I've had an overwhelming feeling to tell her to come back, so I ignore her texts instead for now.

Lottie comes running back to me. "Can we go to our room now? I want to see the top floor."

I chuckle. "Sure. Let's go."

Felix waves, and I give him a nod before walking to the elevator with Lottie.

"Dad? Can we call mum when we get upstairs?" Lottie asks.

"Of course." I nod.

We get into the suite, and it's immaculate. Lottie runs around, touching things that are probably worth more than I have in the bank.

"Careful now, lovie. Don't want to break anything," I say, and she stops touching the glass flowers that are placed in an expensive-looking vase. "Let's call mum."

I hit Caroline's number, and the phone rings for what seems like forever till her voicemail picks up.

"Sorry, baby. Looks like she's busy," I say, and Lottie bursts into tears.

She throws herself into my lap, and I rub her back. "How about I get Natalie to give her a call before you come to the show tonight?"

"Okay." She sits up and wipes her eyes.

"How about you go lay down and take the iPad with you?" I suggest.

"Yes!" She smiles and runs off to a bedroom after digging around in my laptop bag for the iPad. I don't care what any parenting blog says—iPads are a godsend.

After a few hours of relaxing in our room and after a hot shower for me while Lottie slept, we head to the lobby to meet Natalie. I sling Lottie's pink backpack over my shoulder and hold her hand as we get into the elevator. Who knew bad boy Knox Bryan could ever be Mr. Mom? I'm sure some people wouldn't believe it still. Maybe I have been too hard on Mick.

"Hi Nat," Lottie calls to her when we get into the main lobby area.

People turn around to stare at us as we walk by. This pink backpack must really look good. I hand Natalie Lottie's bag, and she smiles at us.

"Hey, Lottie. Are you excited to hang out?" She grins.

I will say this for Natalie; she's quite bubbly and outgoing. She's only been around Lottie since this morning, and Lottie is already her biggest fan.

"Yeah!" Lottie shouts.

"Perf—" Natalie stumbles and trips over someone's suitcase.

"Are you all right?" I reach for her, and she grabs my hand.

"Yeah, just embarrassed." She blushes.

"It's okay. Dad fell off stage a few months ago." Lottie shrugs.

"Thanks for that, Lottie." I laugh.

Natalie starts to limp a bit.

"Are you sure you're good?" I frown.

"My ankle is a bit sore, but I'm sure—ow." She winces.

"Why don't I walk you guys to the restaurant next door? You can have a bite to eat and rest your ankle?"

"Sure, that sounds lovely." Natalie smiles and loops her arm in mine so I can help her walk next door.

"There's an iPad in Lottie's bag, so give that to her, and your job will immediately become easier." I chuckle.

Lottie holds my other hand, and we get out onto the sidewalk in front of the hotel.

Snap. Snap. Snap.

Camera flashes flicker. *Shit.* The paps have found out where we're staying. That's got to be some kind of record.

I can't hear anything they're saying because, between the fans and the reporters, it's hard to distinguish what people are saying. We walk through the crowd and get into the restaurant. I'm so grateful for how close it is. I say goodbye to the girls and go back to get into the SUV that's waiting for me. Walking back through the crowd, more flashes and questions are shouted, but I only pick up on one.

"Knox, what's your wife going to think of you holding hands with a younger woman?" The reporter's accent is American. Maybe that's why it sticks out amongst the sea of Danish paparazzi.

My blood runs cold as I jump into the black car. *Fuck.* Caroline's interpretation hadn't even crossed my mind. My phone starts to ring, and my wife's name flashes on the screen. I let it go to voicemail, unsure of what I should tell her or if I should. We're in Denmark, what are the chances it'll even hit American media? I shake my head. *You idiot.* I had heard the American accent already. It'll be splashed all over the papers by morning.

This is going to be bad.

15

CAROLINE

Rick asked me to check on Mick this morning—he hasn't been answering his phone. Something I know well. Knox replied to only one of my texts last night and didn't call me back any of the four times I called him. The new nanny, Natalie, at least called to let me talk to Lottie. Natalie seems lovely, and Lottie adores her.

When I get to Mick's room, there's a loud scuffle coming from inside, and the door is propped open a bit, so I walk in. Mick and Brandon are locked in what looks like a wrestling move.

"Boys!" I yell. Knowing I can't do this myself, I remember whose door is closest to this room. "Conner!" Conner comes out of his room and is confused for a moment before he rushes inside. He pulls Mick back before he can hit Brandon again. I walk straight to B.

"Are you okay?" I ask him.

"Is he all right? What about me?" Mick spits. Conner continues to restrain him.

"Yeah, I'm fine," Brandon says.

"Let me go!" Mick shouts at Conner, but he doesn't loosen his grip. I help Brandon up.

"Are you going to calm down?" Conner asks.

"I'm fine," Mick says as Conner releases him. Brandon leaves Mick's room without looking back, and Conner trails after him.

"What the fuck happened?" I growl.

"He was in my space and doesn't know how to fucking listen," Mick says as he takes a sip of water from the glass beside his bed.

"You can't go around beating the shit out of your band."

"I can do whatever the fuck I want, and don't forget it. Get out."

"You can't do whatever you want. When are you going to get it?" I say, then sit beside him. "What's going on?"

"Honestly, Caroline, my issues are way more than you could ever imagine." He rubs his eyes.

"Look, you're not perfect. Nobody is but this is something you need to deal with. Candice didn't come back to our room last night, so I'm assuming it has something to do with the same thing?" I say and put a hand on his back. I am shocked he doesn't ask me to remove it immediately.

"Candice didn't go back to your room. That doesn't make sense."

"She texted me and said she was hanging out with a friend, and I shouldn't worry because it wasn't you, so I assumed you had done something." I put my hand on his knee.

"I told her my parents were dead, and they're not."

"Why?"

"Because I wish they fucking were sometimes, okay?" He stands up and runs a hand through his hair.

I let out a sigh. As someone with complicated parents, I understand what he means. My parents haven't talked to me in years because I decided to stay with Knox, and even before then, they weren't stellar parents. "You may not believe me, but I know how you feel."

"Do you now? Somehow, I doubt it very much."

"You think my life has been complete roses? Not even close. My parents were absent most of my life, and you already know the shit I've been through with Knox, so yes, I do have some clue," I say, still sitting on his bed.

"At least Knox loves you and would do anything for you," he says.

His outburst catches me off guard. I don't want to tell him that I'm not so sure about that or about the creeping feeling that Knox is doing something bad again is starting to settle into my bones. "You may not realize it, but Candice will forgive you. She cares about you no matter how unlikely it seems right now."

"She needs to stay away from me. You need to make sure she stays away from me," Mick says.

"You don't want that."

"Yes, I do. I don't want to see her."

"She works for you." I sigh. This is the problem with tour romances. Especially if one person can't admit they're head over heels for the other.

"I'll hire someone else."

"This is the wrong move." I stand up.

"No, it's the right one," he says. "Now, if you wouldn't mind, I need to get ready for practice."

"All right," I say. "Do you need anything before I go?"

"Nope," he says and sits down on his bed again.

I shut the door behind me with a click—the sound of shattering glass echoes in the hallway and causes me to jump. The best thing for him right now is to let him go.

I haven't stopped running around all day, and exhaustion is working its way through my body. Mick's incident has stirred so much drama that my entire day is spent dealing with the crew, Rick, and the other boys.

"Hey, big guy. How are you feeling?" I ask Brandon as he ices his lip.

"Like I was punched in the face." He tries to smile but winces. His face looks bad.

"Are you going to be okay to play?" I ask.

"I'll be fine. I've played through worse. The good thing about being a drummer," he says.

"Has Hannah seen your face yet?" I ask.

"No—I don't want her to see me this way." He sighs and places the ice beside him.

"I get it, but it'll be hard to hide." I sit across from him.

"I don't know how much longer I can do this." His tone is low, and he clasps his hands in front of him.

"Hide from her? Not long, I'd imagine," I say.

"No, Caroline. I mean, be around Mick. We can't keep fighting each other."

"I know." I pause. This is someone he probably thought was going to be his best friend forever, and now they're at odds. It kind of reminds me of Knox and Felix. "Let's take it day by day, all right?"

"Yeah," he gives me a small smile.

"Brandon?" Hannah opens the door but stops when she sees his face. "Babe, what happened?"

"It was a fight with Mick. Not a big deal," he says.

"It is a big deal. You look awful." She picks up the ice and holds it to his lip. This woman is stunning. Her long brown hair is styled with perfect beach waves, and she's dressed in a beautiful shift dress. She could say she just left a runway, and I'd believe it without hesitation.

"It looks worse than what it is." He smiles. "Oh, Hannah, this is my tour manager and friend Caroline. Caroline, this is my lovely girlfriend, Hannah. I realize you guys haven't been properly introduced yet."

"Hi! It's so lovely to meet you."

"You too! Hopefully, everything B has said about me is flattering." Her posh London accent is as gorgeous as she is.

"Of course I do," he says, and she kisses him. "Ow."

"Sorry!" She gasps.

"It's fine." He waves her off.

"I'm going to kill that asshole. Who the hell does he think he is? I'll kill him, Brandon. I don't care how important he thinks he is." She wrings her hands.

"I one hundred percent see why Brandon loves you. You're amazing."

"She's a lot like you," Brandon says.

"That is the best compliment I've gotten in a while." I smile. "All right, I'll leave you two. See you both later." My phone rings.

"Caroline speaking," I answer and get into the hallway.

"Caroline speaking? Did you not check your caller ID before you answered?" Knox asks.

"It's been a weird day," I say and get into the temporary office I set my stuff up in. It's more like an unused conference room, but it has WIFI so I can't complain.

"Elaborate?" he says.

"Mick and Brandon got into a physical fight this morning. Brandon's face is pretty busted up, and now I'm worried B is going to walk away."

"Shit, that's not good. I'm sorry, babe."

"Thanks. I miss you." I slump in my office chair. "How's Lottie? I miss her too."

"She's doing great. I hired a new nanny for the tour. Her name is Natalie," he says.

"I know, she called with Lottie. Why didn't you call me back?" I ask.

"I got caught up. I'm sorry." His answer doesn't satisfy me, but I don't press.

"It's okay." *What the hell is going on with him?* "So, is this new nanny pretty?"

"She's not you."

"That's not a no." I laugh.

"I don't think she's pretty, but Danny does if that helps."

"Well, Danny thinks everyone is pretty." Danny has hooked up with pretty much everyone who's looked his way.

"Remember that I love you." I smile. I've never worried about Knox and a nanny, but I have to tease him.

"And I love you."

"Good. Keep that in mind when we're four months in, and the hot nanny starts giving you the eyes." I giggle.

"The eyes? Wow, very PG of you." He chuckles.

"I should go. I have to go talk to Mick," I say.

"Wait. How's Candice?" he asks.

"She's okay—" I say. I can't lie to him again.

"That's it?"

"She didn't stay with me last night." I brace myself for his reaction.

"Where was she?"

"She said she was hanging out with Conner and then fell asleep on his couch."

"Uh-huh."

"Knox..."

"I didn't say anything."

"I know you, though."

"I only hope she's being careful."

"Me too. I gotta go."

"Love you," he says.

"Love you too. Call me later?" I ask.

"Will do."

We say our goodbyes, and I hang up. I saunter down the hall towards Mick's dressing room. The knots in my stomach are tightening. I'd rather be doing anything else. I knock on his door. Better get this over with as quickly as possible.

"Hey Mick, I…" I stop when I see a young girl next to him, "Oh, hello there. I'm Caroline."

"Hi. I'm Violet." She holds out her hand, and I shake it.

"My sister."

"Oh! That's great. Nice to meet you! Are you going to be with us long?" I ask.

"Till Thursday," she says.

"Welcome." I smile. "Mick, can I talk to you for a second?"

"Sure. Vi, go find Brandon. I think he's down the hallway," Mick says.

"Cool! Later, Caroline." She waves as she leaves.

"You're sending her to see Brandon?" I ask and sit on the couch.

"She's known him as long as I have." He shrugs and sits on the opposite couch.

"How are you doing?" I ask with apprehension, unsure if he's about to throw another glass.

"Fine. Uh—how is Brandon?" If I didn't know any better, I'd say he cares.

"He's all right. His lip is pretty beaten up. Look, we need to fix things between you guys or he's going to end up leaving."

"I know." Mick looks down at his hands.

"I don't understand why you guys can't work it out. This is all over a fight that you had two years ago?" I ask.

"It's more than that," he says.

"How?" I cross my arms. He's not going to get away with shutting down again.

"It just is."

"We're having another band meeting to figure this out."

"I know I fucked up—in more ways than one." He lets out a breath.

"Have you talked to her?" I ask.

"Yeah, a bit. She's already been nice to me even though she shouldn't be," he says.

"That's Candice. Always forgiving and always understanding," I reply. Candice has the biggest heart of anyone I know. Mick gets up and starts to write.

"What are you doing?" I ask.

"Something. I'll see you later, yeah?" He's brushing me off.

"Sounds good. Band meeting at four," I say as I stand.

He nods but doesn't look up from his notebook.

A few hours later, all of us are back in Rick's hotel room. Talk about Déjà Vu.

"Okay, so where shall we start?" Rick says as he looks at the five of them.

Rick and I are sitting opposite of the boys. Mick is jammed between Kane and Tommy, a move that isn't unintentional.

"Our morale is shit," Kane says.

"Extreme shit," Tommy agrees.

"I'm sorry," Mick mumbles while playing with the ring on his index finger.

"What?" Kane says.

Brandon stands up and moves closer to him. Rick goes to stand, but I place my hand on his forearm.

"After all the shit this guy has done, we're supposed to sit here and accept his apology and say everything is good? Everything is grand? No fucking way. He hasn't got a care for anything. Not this band. Not himself. Anything." Brandon's veins are popping out his neck.

"Brandon!" I say.

"I don't expect you to believe me, but I'm serious," Mick says. He and Brandon are locked in a stare-down.

"What brought on this big change? What has made you see the light? You woke up and decided you're not going to be a dick anymore?" He crosses his arms.

"No reason." Mick shrugs. "I want to continue the success we have with all of us. Maybe you don't believe me, and that's fine. After the past few years, I get it, but you out of everyone here, you were like my brother in the beginning."

"Your brother, who you beat the shit out of this morning for no reason." Brandon glares.

"I can never take it back—nor can I take back anything that's happened in the past, but I can promise to try and be better," Mick says.

Brandon moves closer to Mick, making every hair on my arm stand straight up. This is either going to be good or incredibly bad. He grabs Mick and pulls him in for a hug. I send up a silent prayer.

They whisper something to each other and then smile. This is the first time I feel like I belong here and that I'm making a difference.

"Now, this is all out of the way." Rick wipes a tear away from his eye. "Let's really get started."

"Rick! Are you crying, mate?" Conner laughs.

"No. Shut up." He wipes his eyes again.

This is how the tour should be, and I'm stoked to be a part of it.

The first show was amazing. Mick and the lads were fantastic. They were all so excited. They hugged at the end of the stage. Rick rented the top floor of a lounge in Manhattan. I'm not much of a partier, but I go to see everyone.

"To the first of many successful dates on the rest of the tour!" Rick raises his glass and we all cheers.

"Hey, lovely," I say to Candice. She had snuck into our room this morning, but she told me she slept again on Conner's couch. Except there's no way that happened. Between Mick's good mood and the grin on Candice's face, I suspect they were together.

"Hey." She smiles.

"What a great show, yeah?" I say over the music.

"Yeah, it was so good! Even better than London," she says.

Everyone is chatting amongst their little groups. Mick is standing with Violet, Tommy, and Conner. Violet is looking at Conner like he's the only thing that exists. Mick might have some trouble on his hands with that.

"Must have something to do with their newfound friendship," I say.

"How are you doing?"

"Good. Missing my family."

"I get it. Only a few more weeks, right? We head to New Jersey for two shows, then Boston for two, then Chicago for one, right?"

"Yup, that's the plan. Two nights at each with two to three days in between for travel and free time."

We catch up some more, chatting about groupies before we're pulled into a group hug by Conner.

"There are my girls!" Conner says.

"Conner!" Candice says. "Great show."

"Thanks, darlin'," he says.

"You were fantastic," I say.

"I know. Must have something to do with the new vibes," he says.

"Yeah, they are rocking. Hey, I meant to say earlier way to keep stealing my best friend from me." I tease him. They have been spending quite a bit of time together.

"I'm quite charming Caroline, but I don't think having dinner with her counts as stealing," he says.

"What? She was gone all night." My eyes narrow at Candice. While I could guess where she was, now I'm as worried as Knox is about her making the wrong decisions.

"Not with me, my dear! Oh, Kane—sorry ladies, I gotta catch up to him." Conner gives us one last smile before he heads off.

"Where were you last night?" I ask. My tone is similar to one that I give Lottie when she's lying to me.

"Huh? I can't hear you over the music," she says.

"Where were you?" I say louder.

"Oh—I was uh—I was with Mick."

"Candice. This isn't good. This is your job here."

"It wasn't planned."

"It never is! Candice, I thought you were going to take this seriously." I cross my arms. If Rick fires her, then I'm on my own, and she's back to London.

"I went with my gut, which is what you always tell me to do."

"So, what's going on now? You're sleeping together or what?"

"I don't know. I—I don't know."

"Figure it out. You need to tell Rick if something is going to keep happening," I say.

"I know." She wrings her hands.

"Good," I say.

"Really?" Her jaw drops.

"Really. You're an adult, Candy. I'm going to go find Rick. I'll talk to you later?"

"Sounds good. I might head back soon. I'm still feeling the jet lag," she says.

"Text me, so I know you're not dead." I hug her then make my way back through the crowd.

I'm ready to enjoy my night and blow off some steam.

"Caroline? Have you talked to Knox?" Rick grabs me by the arm.

"No, why?" I ask.

Rick hands me his phone, and there's a photo of Knox and some woman with Lottie. Knox and the woman have looped arms, and he's laughing. They look like a picture-perfect couple. Except he's my husband, and that's definitely not me. Is this the reason he's been so distant?

I dial his number, but it goes straight to voicemail like it has been all day. The only time he stopped returning my calls before is when—but that can't be, can it? Has my husband relapsed?

My mind is racing. One thing is for sure, I need to talk to my husband now.

16

KNOX

The pictures online and splashed on every tabloid are bad. Very bad. It looks like I've replaced Caroline with an extremely younger model. There wasn't much time to react to them. As soon as the show in Copenhagen was done, we took a flight to Oslo, where I'm currently waiting for my parents to show up. Our concert in Oslo isn't for two days, but we came early to get set up and have some sense of normalcy for longer than twelve hours. Caroline has called multiple times, but I can't answer. I don't want to tell her about this and have her worry about something else. She probably already knows.

"Knox! Lottie!" My ma calls out to me.

"Poppy! Nana!" Lottie lets go of my hand and runs towards them, then launches herself in my Da's arms.

Alan and Cynthia Bryan, next to Lottie and Caroline, are my two biggest fans. Even when I was going through all my shit with drugs, they never gave up on me. They're the reason I'm the parent I am. I've always wanted to be a father like my Da. My Da is as tall as me with the same brown hair. Candice and I get our eyes from our Ma. She's the beauty in the family, for sure.

"Good to see you, Knox." My Da slaps me on the shoulder after placing Lottie back down on two feet.

"You too. How was the flight?" I ask.

"The same as it always is. Quick. No fuss. Thanks for getting the flight for us." My Ma smiles and pulls me in for a hug.

"Any time," I say. "Ma, I was wondering if you'd be all right hanging out with Lottie so I can have a quick chat with Da. Here's the key. Your room is right beside mine—3104."

"Of course! We can go get ready for dinner, right, Lottie?" she says.

"Yeah!" Lottie cheers. They walk hand and hand to the elevator.

"Shall we take a seat, son?" My Da asks.

"Yeah, let's get a table." I motion for the host, and he seats us in a private booth, away from prying ears.

"What's going on, Knox? Have you relapsed? Cause if ya have, it's okay. We can get you the help you need." Concern crosses his features.

"It's not that." I sigh. "The nanny—Lottie's—Natalie, she fell, so I helped her walk to the restaurant next door. Lottie is there too. It looks like we're together. The photos."

"Has anything happened with the nanny?" He asks.

"No. Never. You know I'd never do that. Even in my darkest moments, I've never cheated on Caroline." I shake my head.

"Then what? It's some pictures. There have been many of you in compromising positions before." He strokes his chin.

He's not wrong. There have been so many pictures over the past few years that it's not like this is completely new for us.

"I know. You're right."

"I guess I'm not seeing the issue if you've talked to Caroline about it."

"I haven't. She's been gone less than a week, and this happened. I don't want her to doubt me or us," I say.

"Knox. I love you, but you're daft. What else is going on?" His eyes bounce back and forth, trying to read my face.

"I—there's something else."

"You don't say." He winks at me.

"I think maybe I'm done with music. I'm tired. And—" How do I tell him the truth about my mental health? I haven't even admitted it to myself yet.

"You can tell me anything." He places a hand over mine.

"I might have depression or something. I don't know. Even before Caroline left, I've been struggling to write this album. It's not perfect enough. My anxiety about, well, everything has been through the roof. I think it's all finally wore me down. But I'm functioning, so I don't get it." There's an instant weight that lifts off my shoulders.

My Da slides next to me and puts an arm around my shoulders, then squeezes. I hang my head and let one tear slide down my cheek. This battle has been mine alone for so long. Roberto knew something was going on but not to this extent. Caroline looks at me as her hero for the past few years. How can I tell her we have another battle to face?

"Your Ma and I have known about the anxiety since you were a child. We may have failed you a bit. But back then, no one really knew how to handle it. It's something that the world has finally acknowledged and provided support for it over the last few years," he says.

"True. I can't be the poster child of this too. When will things stop? When will I be fucking normal?" The anger twists in my stomach. How is this another cross I have to bear?

"All right, now you're pitying yourself." He smiles and pats my shoulder. "You are completely normal with an extraordinary gift and platform. If someone else said this to you, would you tell them that they're a failure? You wouldn't. You'd give them empathy. So do that for yourself now."

"I'm so tired and so old. I feel slices and cuts in my soul. And it all feels bleak Da, it really does." I stare at my hands on the table.

"Now, look at me. Open your eyes. You have an opportunity many don't. Get help with this. You did it for the drugs, do it now for depression. You will be okay, Knox." He wraps both arms around me now and hugs me.

A few more tears spill down my cheeks before I wipe them away. I sniff. "What do I do now?"

"Go to New York and tell your wife. You need her, and it's okay to need her." He shuffles out of the booth and gestures me to stand.

"What about Lottie?" I ask.

"We have her. The benefit of being retired, we can stay as long as you need."

We walk to the elevator and get in. When we get to our floor, I let Ma know, and I call the airline to grab a flight out in the next few hours to New York.

I unlock my room door, and my eyes are adjusting to the darkness when I hear a voice from behind me.

"Knox, you scared me." Natalie is standing in the middle of my suite, and I flick on the light. I had given her a key this morning, but I told her to take off the rest of the day.

"What are you doing in here?" I ask. My heart is thumping. Where in the hell did this lass come from?

"Oh. Did you see the papers?" She asks and sits on one of the couches.

"Yes, I'm terribly sorry for getting you messed up in all of this—hazards of working for someone like me. I'll get my publicist to take care of it," I say. "Hopefully, this doesn't have you rethinking the job."

"Oh no." She shakes her head.

"Good. Anyways Natalie, I have to—"

"It's actually making me think that maybe if you're interested, we could start something privately. A gorgeous man like you must have women everywhere. We make a cute couple I think." She smiles.

What the fuck.

I shake my head. "I think you've gotten the wrong impression of me. I've never cheated on my wife, and I never will."

"Never say never." She stands and moves closer to me.

"Never. I would never," I say. I know I have to fire her, but I don't want to deal with this now. I want her to leave.

Natalie moves quickly and plants a kiss on my lips. I grab her by the wrists and move her away from me.

"You need to go. You're fired. I'll get someone to get you a flight home." My voice is louder than I had intended.

"I—I thought this is what you wanted." Her brows scrunch together.

"No. If you leave now, we don't need to talk about this again," I say, and she nods. She grabs her purse that is lying on the floor and leaves my suite. Nothing matters except getting to Caroline.

After packing and booking a flight, I let my parents know that I'm going to New York. I also let them know that Natalie is fired and what happened in my hotel room. There's so much time to think on the flight that I turn on my music and try to sleep.

When we land, I'm buzzing to get to Caroline. I am so ready to see and hold her. I have four more missed calls from her. She's got to be proper pissed. Their show would have ended not too long ago, so it's almost perfect timing to arrive.

I text Rick, who sends me the details of Caroline's room. They're all heading out for dinner tonight. My knuckles rap on the door, and Caroline answers.

"Knox?" Her voice is barely a whisper.

"It's me," I say.

"Where's Lottie?" She asks, not moving. She pinches me.

"Ow!"

"Sorry, just checking you're real." She giggles.

"She's in Oslo with Ma and Da."

She wraps her arms around me and holds me tight for a moment. Her smell of vanilla and bergamot fills my nose. This is what home feels like.

"I can't believe you're here." The tears start to form in her eyes. She steps back and lets me into her room. "I can't believe you're here, and I'm so fucking angry at you."

Even though I knew it was coming, I had missed too many phone calls for her not to be mad. It still stings. She sits on the bed, and I lean against the TV stand.

"It's not what it looks like." I rub my face.

"Really, Knox? That's the best you have after flying all this way? Come on." She crosses her arms.

"I know. She fell, and I helped her up. Then she was limping, so I offered her my arm. It's not what it's been made out to be," I say.

"Then why are you here? If this is what it is—why are you here?" she asks.

Tell her. Tell her everything. "The truth is—she hit on me, but I fired her."

There really isn't a real reason to get into it fully.

Caroline swallows. "Okay. You haven't relapsed?"

"What? No! Of course not." I say, and Caroline visibly relaxes. "You thought I was here to tell you I need to go to rehab again?"

"The last time you avoided my calls, you were on a bender. I was considering booking a flight to get to you and Lottie. I was worried, but Felix said that's not what's going on—"

"You called Felix?" I ask. The heat rises to my face.

"I didn't know what else to do! You left me zero options, Knox. You didn't reply to most of my texts. Your calls have been brief. I needed to make sure Lottie was okay, that you were okay."

The anger melts away. It makes sense. I'd do the same thing.

"How long are you here for?" she asks.

"The day after tomorrow. I have to get on a flight at three in the morning, though," I say. "My parents said they could bring Lottie over for a few days."

Tears spring into her eyes. "I'd love that. Thank you."

"Of course." I smile. Maybe it's selfish, but I also need some time alone to sort through the shit going on inside of me.

Caroline's phone beeps. "I forgot I said I'd go to dinner with everyone."

"Right. I'll take a quick shower and meet you there, all right?" I ask.

"Sounds good." Caroline gives me a quick hug before leaving.

Before getting into the shower, I sit on the edge of the bed and hang my head. I had the chance to tell her the truth, but I couldn't. I'm a coward.

After the shower, I head out of the hotel room with fresh clothes and feel a bit more alive. It's extremely late, but in New York, the streets are still buzzing. Most people don't even go to dinner till ten.

"Knox?" I turn to see a man approaching me. He's in his late 50s and is wearing all black. He looks vaguely familiar.

"Sorry, do I know you?" I ask.

"We've met a few times. I'm Rex, Mick's bodyguard." He holds out his hand, and I shake it.

"How do you handle that?" I ask with a chuckle.

"Ah, he's really not that bad. If you let him, he'll surprise you." He shrugs.

"That's a bit hard to believe for me. And now, with him dating my sister, it's going to be even harder not to be tough on him," I say.

"You do realize you were his hero, right?"

Rex's comment catches me off guard. "What do you mean?"

"I mean for a long time you were the poster he had in his room. You were who he wanted to be. He even went to meet you when he was a wee lad, but you weren't exactly welcoming."

"I don't remember. When was that?" I ask.

"Mick had to have been about sixteen." Rex scratches his chin.

It had to have been during one of my relapses. "Shit. No wonder he hated recording with me. I was a complete asshole when I was high."

"Yeah, you were. But everyone else gave you a second chance. Maybe you can extend the same courtesy." He gives me a nod before he heads towards the elevator.

As much as I hate to admit it, he's right. Maybe I do need to give Mick a chance.

The restaurant is packed, but I go through the back entrance that Caroline texted me about. I'm not interested in crowds currently or more speculation as to why I'm in New York.

"Hello," I say when I get to the group.

"Knox!" Candice's eyes bug out of her head as she rushes over to give me a big hug. Everyone calls out their hellos as well.

"Hi, Candy," I say as we embrace. "What have you done to your hair? I like it."

"It's something new I thought I'd try." She runs a hand through it. "Who's watching Lottie?"

"Mum and Da," I say, taking the seat that's free next to Mick.

"Knox." Mick nods.

I'm not shocked by the icy reception. Especially now after what Rex had said. "How are ya holdin' up?"

"Uh, good," Mick flinches, clearly not used to me being anything but confrontational. He asks Candice. "Did you know he was here?"

She shakes her head.

"He got here this evening. Long story." Caroline takes a sip of her drink.

"Girls, can you excuse us, please? Mick and I are going to go outside quick." This is my time to make things right with him.

"Uhm—" Candice goes to protest, but Caroline stops her.

"Sure," Caroline says.

Mick and I stand and head outside to the private back patio. It's surrounded by red brick buildings and is an odd little oasis in the middle of a concrete jungle.

"What's up with the private chat?" Mick asks as he stuffs his hands into his leather jacket. For a second, he looks like a kid, one who got the brunt of my anger for no reason.

"I'm sorry." I let out a breath, and Mick coughs.

"What?" he asks. "You are?"

"Yes. Rex told me what happened when we met a few years ago when I saw him in the lobby this afternoon, and now I get why you were such an insufferable prick the entire time we were recording 'My Amazing Girl,'" I say.

"Ah, did he?" His eyes narrow, clearly uncomfortable with the vulnerability. Maybe we have more in common than I realize.

"Don't be mad at him. He was defending you and telling me I needed to give you a chance."

"I don't need it."

"For Candice's sake, maybe we should get along?"

"Maybe," he says. I don't blame him for being cautious.

"I get we're never going to be mates, but I'm going to look out for the best interests of my sister. She picked you, and that's a lot of responsibility," I say.

"How so?" he frowns.

"Candice isn't someone you let go of easily. She'll love you more than anyone ever will, and she has a huge heart, don't take advantage of it." I smile. Candice is like Caroline in that way. It's the reason I know that love is life-changing for people like me and people like Mick.

"I won't." His eyes dart back and forth, lost in thought.

"Good. I'm not going to say I'm happy you're together because I'm not," I say, "but I'm glad she's happy."

"Can I ask you something?" he asks.

"Sure."

"When you were fucked up on cocaine all the time, did you care about anything?"

"What do you mean?"

"Like Caroline or your kid?"

"I haven't done cocaine or had a drink since before Lottie was born," I say. "But I did care about Caroline, but not as much as getting high back then. Why?"

"Just asking." He kicks at the ground.

"Do you ever want to quit? Get out of the business?" With him opening up, it makes me feel like I can too a bit.

"No. Not at all, actually. I love making music," he says.

I nod. Of course, he didn't. Why would anyone give up this once-in-a-lifetime chance that people literally break their necks over?

"Why? You thinking about quitting, mate?" He asks.

"No," I say. "Not entirely."

"What?"

"I'm trying to figure some stuff out."

"I'd love it if you'd quit. It'd give us a chance to be the number one band out of the UK for a while."

"You wish." I laugh.

Candice bursts through the door. "I don't care, Caroline. They're gone too long I think they're…" She trails off when she sees us staring at her. "Fighting."

"We're not," I say.

"You're not fighting?" Candice asks.

"Not at all?" Caroline finishes.

"Relax, we're not best mates," Mick says.

"But we're not trying to kill each other," I say.

"Already finishing each other sentences? How cute," Caroline teases.

"All right, all right. Glad you're good, Mick. Dinner tomorrow after the show?" I look at Caroline then Mick.

"Are you inviting me?" Mick smirks.

"I guess I am," I say. "We'll wait for you two in the lobby tomorrow."

I grab Caroline's hand and head back inside.

"That was nice of you." Caroline eyes me carefully as we get back to the table. Everyone else is so lost in their own conversations they aren't listening to ours.

"I'm happy to be here, and I want to spend time with you and Candice. That means Mick." I shrug.

Caroline stares at me for a second longer before she looks down at her menu. She grabs my hand, and even though we haven't worked things out, I'm happy she's not mad at me anymore.

"How's everything going tonight?" Mick shouts at the crowd, and they answer him with a roar of applause.

I'm standing next to Candice and Caroline, feeling the insane energy from the audience. When he approached me about this idea earlier, I had agreed, but now the anxiety in my chest is causing me to think twice.

"Good!" Mick smiles. "I am so happy to be here tonight!" More screaming as he grabs my acoustic guitar. The rest of the lads exit the stage, and Brandon slaps me on the back as Conner hands me his acoustic guitar.

"I'm going to play a song you all know with a special guest tonight," Mick says. "Ladies and gentlemen, please put your hands together for Mr. Knox Bryan!" The crowd goes insane.

I walk out with the guitar. I shoot a look back at Candice and Caroline, who are staring with their mouths open. Their sound tech mics me up quickly, and I sit on the stool beside Mick.

"Hi, everyone." I wave to the crowd.

"All right, Knox, can you please tell the crowd what we're going to play for them tonight?" Mick asks.

"It's a little hit called 'My Amazing Girl,'" I say as the crowd goes wild again. "I wrote this song for my wife Caroline, and I have to say I'm so proud with how The Talons have made it their own."

"Thank you," he says, "so this next one goes to Knox's wife Caroline, the inspiration behind it, and to my girlfriend Candice, my inspiration from now on."

I smile at Mick, and he starts to strum.

We finish playing, and I give one more wave to the crowd before exiting the stage. Caroline and Candice beam at me. This is the best I've felt in so long.

17

CAROLINE

Knox and Mick are becoming friends, and it's freaking me out. Even though I've had my own breakthrough with him, it's still weird. Knox showing up has been so great, but something is going on that I can't put my finger on. If he says he's clean, I believe him. If he says he didn't hook up with the nanny, I believe him. But if he says everything is all right, well that's another story.

We're standing in the lobby waiting for Candice and Mick. Knox laces his fingers through mine and smiles at me. There's a distance in his eyes.

"Knox—" I start.

"Hey guys," Candice says.

It's not the time to have this conversation. Maybe when we get to Paris. "Let's go. I'm starving."

Candice holds her stomach. "Me too, apparently."

Rex gives us a lift to a quiet little restaurant not too far from our hotel. We walk inside, and it's empty.

"Hello," the hostess greets us. "We kept the restaurant empty for you all so you can have your meal in privacy."

"Thank you so much," Knox says.

"Not a problem. Right, this way." We sit at a booth with Mick and

Candice on one side and Knox and me on the other. It's weird to think the last time we were all together, how badly it ended.

"Your parents are calling me." I frown. "Hello? Hi Lottie… I'm out with Mick and Aunt Candy and Daddy. How's Nana and Poppy?" I get up from the table.

"Hi, mum!" Lottie's voice makes me instantly smile. "Nana and Poppy are great. But my friend Natalie is gone. She was so fun."

Too bad she wanted to play house with your father. "Oh really? That's too bad."

"Anyways, miss you, mom! Here's Poppy." She hands the phone to her grandfather.

"Hi, beauty." Alan's voice comes over the phone.

"Hi Alan! How are things?" I ask.

"Oh good, good. She's being a little firecracker as usual. She's more like Knox than we realized because she got all of your good looks." He chuckles.

"You flatter me," I say.

"Listen, I think it's good Knox is there. I think you guys can really work together to get him the help he needs," Alan says.

"The help he needs?" I repeat, and my blood runs cold.

"Yeah, with the depression—did he tell you?" He asks.

"Of course." I clear my throat. It's all starting to click. "Listen, I have to go, Alan! Thanks again for taking care of Lottie. Love you guys."

"Love you too!" Alan hangs up.

Knox has depression but hasn't told me. How can we be so solid yet so fractured at the same time? I shake my head and head back into the restaurant.

"Awesome," Mick says.

"What's awesome?" I say as I rejoin them.

"Mick is going to come to London after the Boston show to help me out with the album," Knox says.

"Really?" I raise my eyebrows.

"Yup," Knox says.

"You guys are best friends now?" I ask.

"I don't think so," Mick says.

"We're helping each other out. I mean, it's the least old Mick can do for me, seeing as how I wrote their number one single right now," Knox teases.

"I'll repay the favour then, mate." Mick chuckles.

"This is freaking me out," I say and glance down at the menu. My heart is pumping so hard. I'm trying not to blurt everything out at the table.

"Me too," Candice agrees.

"I thought this would be your dream?" Mick says.

"You two in cahoots? Not likely." She smiles.

"Cahoots? Really?" Mick laughs.

"Sorry, I'm not cool and young like you." Candice sticks her tongue out at him.

Everything around me is starting to blend together. The sounds are mashing into one, and people are rushing by. I focus back on the table and the conversation going on around me.

"I always forget how old you are," Mick says.

"I must be ancient," Knox cuts in.

"Fourteen years older than me." Mick smiles. "I guess only thirteen. I turn twenty-two next month."

"Ugh, twenty-two," I groan. I can be normal. I can get through this. "I remember twenty-two. I miss twenty-two. Are you going to go to London then?"

"Yeah, I think so," Candice replies, "it's good timing because I have to take care of some things."

"Oh?" I ask.

"Change some things for my apartment." She takes a sip of her water.

Felix must have heard about Mick's declaration. My eyes narrow. "He knows, doesn't he?"

"Of course," she says.

"Who knows what?" Mick frowns.

"Felix," Candice answers.

"Oh. So, I guess he cut you off then?" Mick asks.

"What's that supposed to mean?" Her eyebrows scrunch together.

"You have to go take care of stuff at home, so I assumed it was because he cut you off," he says. "I didn't mean to offend you."

"You did," Candice says. "I want to switch everything into my name."

"All right, all right," I cut in. "Let's switch the subject."

The rest of the dinner passes quickly with a few awkward silences. Thankfully Knox and Mick keep up the conversation as Candice, and I are in our own separate worlds. No doubt she's upset about Mick's comment and me, well, I'm trying to keep myself together.

We get back to the hotel, and Knox sits on the edge of my bed. Candice is with Mick, so it's the two of us.

"We have to talk, Caroline," he says and grabs my hand.

"About?" I ask, feigning innocence.

"About us—" he trails off.

"Are you leaving me?" I pull my hand out of his grasp.

"No, of course not. I love you more than anything. Don't you ever forget that." He pulls me into a hug.

"Then what?"

"I'm not happy."

"But you just said you're not leaving." I search his face. His eyes are tired, and he looks older somehow.

"It's not you," he says. "It's touring. It's being away from my family. I want to have more kids, and I want to be able to see them grow up. I know you and Lottie travel with me, but it's not the same. She's with the nanny or you for ten hours a day, and when I do see her, it's for an hour before she sleeps."

"More kids?" My stomach tightens.

"Don't you want that?" he asks.

"I—" I hesitate. Of course, I did but not soon. "Yes, but not now. I want to be able to do this job for at least a few tours. "Plus, you love music."

"I love music, but I love you and Lottie more. I don't want to be in different time zones all the time."

"It's only been a week, and already you've changed your mind about supporting me and my career ambitions?" My blood boils.

"What? Absolutely not. That's not what this is."

"Then what? What else could there possibly be that you're not saying?" I ask.

He doesn't say anything and looks at the floor. I'm being too harsh.

With the new information Alan threw into my lap earlier, we need to cool off.

"Knox, this is a lot to take in," I say.

"I know. I don't know what to do," he says.

"Why do we have to make this decision today? Right now?" I ask.

"We don't," he replies.

He moves up towards the headboard and kicks off his shoes. I follow suit and wrap my arms around him.

We're in trouble, and neither of us knows how to deal with it.

Knox left, and we finished off the concerts in New York and Boston. Candice and Mick left earlier today to go meet up with Knox in London so I'm on my own. Knox and I haven't figured anything out, mostly because I still haven't mentioned anything that Alan said to me.

"Dinner?" Brandon knocks on my door. Hannah also went back to London yesterday for the week to visit her family, so he's also alone.

"Yes, please." I nod, putting down my books. We head out of the hotel to an all-night diner close by. Even though Brandon said dinner, it almost made more sense if he had said breakfast. It's still before noon.

"I want a hamburger," I say, scanning the menu.

"Milkshake and fries for me. Lottie gets here tomorrow?" he asks and drums his fingers against the table. Something is going on with him.

"Yeah, she does! I'm so excited," I say. I study Brandon's face. "Are you all right?"

"I—I'm okay," he says.

"You know you can tell me if something's up…" I reach for his hand.

"To be honest, Caroline saying it out loud is going to make it real."

"Hannah's pregnant?"

"No, nothing like that," Brandon looks up at me, and I can see there are tears in his eyes.

"Oh my God, B." I get up and slide into the booth beside him. "What's going on?" I wrap my arm around his shoulders.

"Hannah uhm she's—she's sick," he chokes out.

"Sick? What kind of sick?" I ask.

"She has breast cancer. She went to her doctor a few months ago, and they had found a lump. Before we left, they did a biopsy, and she went back this week to get the results, and she has stage four. Which means it's probably spread to other parts of her body. They'll know more tomorrow."

"Why didn't you go home with Mick and Candice?"

"I don't know. I can't do it. I can't bring myself to go. I'm a horrible person." He dabs his eyes with the back of his hands.

"No, you're not." I rub his back.

"Yes, I am. I can't even bring myself to go home to support the woman I love. I'm a coward." He shakes his head. An idea pops into my mind.

"Wait one minute." I get out of the booth and call Knox.

"Hey," he answers right away. Thankfully this isn't one of the times he doesn't answer my call.

"Hi. Have your parents and Lottie left yet?" I ask.

"No, they leave in a few hours," he says.

"Can you cancel their flights? I'm going to come to London instead and I'm going to leave within the next hour," I reply.

"Is everything okay?" he asks.

"Hannah, Brandon's girlfriend, has cancer, and I don't think Brandon is going to make the whole flight by himself."

"Oh shit. Yeah definitely. We'll see you when you get here," he replies.

"Thanks, bye." I hang up quick before it could get awkward. We haven't talked about anything he said the other night, and now's not the time to dive into it.

I dial Rick's number.

"Hey Caroline," he answers.

"Hi. I need you to do me a huge favour. Can you call any private jet airlines and get one ready? Brandon and I need to leave for London as soon as possible."

"For sure. I can do that right away. Are you two okay?"

"We're fine, but Hannah's sick. We might have to delay the tour."

"Keep me posted. The sooner we know, the better it is to change everything. I'll worry about that. You two get to the airport."

"Thanks, Rick. You're amazing," I say and hang up. I walk back over to the booth, where Brandon has his head in his hands.

"Let's go," I say.

"What do you mean?" he asks.

"We gotta go. The plane should be waiting for us. We're going back to London," I reply.

"I don't think I can," he says.

"Yes, you can. And I'm going to be there too so we can get through this together," I say.

He gets out of the booth and wraps his arms around me. "Thank you so much."

"Of course. Now we gotta pack," I say.

My stomach is in knots as the plane takes off. I was excited to get home to my bed and my kid. My daughter is a month older than the last time I had hugged her.

"I've missed London," Brandon says. It's almost time to land, and he's spent most of the time looking out the window.

"Are you going to be all right?" I ask.

"I don't know. I mean, Hannah has a chance to beat this, but after looking up statistics it…" he pauses and swallows hard. "The odds don't look good."

"Hannah is tough. She can do this," I say.

"We're about to land soon." Brandon changes the subject.

We buckle up. The landing was easy, and it was raining in London. I'm home. I adjust my watch to London time. Knox and Mick were meeting at the studio today to start working on a song. We walk along the tarmac in silence. When we get to the terminal, I grab my bag and notice Pete standing at the front.

"You're going to be okay right?" I ask Brandon.

"I will be." He gives me a small smile. We go to the front of the airport, and I give him a big hug.

"Call me if you need anything. If not, we can meet back here. We can take the same flight as Candice and Mick back. I'll text you the details when I talk to them," I say.

"Thanks, Caroline. I mean it. You're amazing," he says.

"Go get your girl," I smile. He walks away with Trevor and hops into the waiting black SUV.

"Caroline?" I hear from behind me.

"Mummy!" I turn to see my husband and my daughter. They must have been hiding in the car.

"Hi, my baby." I squeeze her.

"Mum, I'm so happy you're home." She grins.

"I am so happy to be here," I kiss the top of her head. Knox walks over to us and pulls us both in for a hug.

"I love you," I say.

"Love you too, mum." Lottie smiles.

"How is the tour, my love?" I ask her.

"Fun!"

"Good."

"Da and Ma are back at the house," Knox says.

"I didn't expect to see you here," I say. Lottie grabs both our hands.

"Lottie really wanted to come." He pauses. "Me too, of course."

"I love you," I say.

"I love you too. How's Brandon?" he asks.

"He's been better. I really hope Hannah is all right," I say.

"Me too." He nods. "Let's go home."

We pull up to our house twenty minutes later. A rush of comfort falls over me as soon as I step inside. I missed this house more than I had thought.

"Caroline, so good to see you, dear." Alan greets me with a hug. Candice is the spitting image of her father. His blonde hair and eyes were clearly mirrored in his daughter. Knox got his height from his dad, though.

"You too!" I reply.

"Cyn come in here," he calls, "Caroline's here." My mother-in-law shuffles out of the kitchen towards me. Cynthia is only an inch shorter than me with curly brown hair.

"It's so good to see you love." Cynthia gives me a hug.

"You too, Cyn," I say.

"You must be exhausted. Would you like some coffee?" she asks.

"Yes, please," I reply.

"Mum, I'm going to go watch TV, okay?" Lottie asks.

"Yes, go ahead," I say. She gives me a giant hug before running off towards the den.

"Knox, come to the kitchen and make your mother and wife some coffee," Cynthia smiles.

"Yes, Ma." He rolls his eyes and walks to the kitchen. Cynthia, Alan, and I follow close behind.

"How was the flight?" Cynthia asks.

"It was good. It went pretty fast. I had a good sleep," I reply.

"Knox told us about your friend Brandon. How awful." Cynthia shakes her head.

"I know. I couldn't imagine," I say. Knox places a pot of coffee in the middle of the kitchen table. He also grabs the cream and sugar before joining us.

"Gosh, and how about the tabloids lately?" Cynthia says.

"Ah yes. I forgot you browse those at the supermarket," I chuckle, "there's no truth to any of it."

"I know, dear. I'm glad that Knox fired that Nanny when he did," she says.

"Ma."

"Sorry, but I'm glad she's gone. I mean kissing you, for gosh sakes. That's ridiculous."

"Kiss?" I frown.

"Oh…" Cynthia says. I look at Knox, who doesn't make eye contact.

"I think Lottie is calling us." Alan quickly stands and motions for Cynthia to follow.

"Now, before you say anything…" Knox says.

"Please. Continue." I cross my arms.

"I fired her." He stands.

"You lied to me."

"No, I didn't," he replies.

"You didn't tell me. Lying by omission is still a fucking lie," I say quietly so his parents and Lottie can't hear us. "Not only that, Knox, but your dad also told me about the depression."

Knox's face goes white. "He did?"

"What else are you keeping from me? Did you cheat on me?" I stand and point my finger at him.

"No. Of course not." He grabs my arm. I wrench it away from him.

"I don't trust you. After all this time that we've been together, after all the shit I've been through with you! Why the hell didn't you tell me?"

"I-I don't know."

"We're in trouble, aren't we?"

"No, we're not. I love you more than anything."

"And I love you too, but Knox, this isn't us. We promised each other we'd always be honest, and this is a big deal."

"It's not that big of a deal. I've been seeing a counsellor. Roberto helped me find her," he says.

My stomach drops. "Roberto knows, your parents know, who else? Am I the only person in the complete dark about what is going on with you? You should have told me about the depression. I have always been there for you, and this is no different. You need to go."

"Caroline, please," he says.

"No. Go to the studio or something. I don't want you around right now." I lean over the kitchen sink, trying to breathe. My entire life is flashing in front of my eyes. This is supposed to be the love of my life. My partner. Now I can't trust anything he says.

"Can I at least come home tonight?"

"The couch is pretty comfy."

"Caroline." he grabs my wrist.

"No, Knox. Not right now," I say. He drops my wrist and turns to leave. I can't catch my breath and sink to the ground. Things are starting to fall apart.

I'm sitting in my kitchen, fidgeting with a loose screw, when my phone rings.

"Hello?" I answer.

"Hey. Can I come over?" Candice asks.

"Yes please." I sniff.

"Are you crying?"

"No."

"Caroline."

"Okay, yes. Knox and I had a blow-up fight. Your parents took Lottie to a movie, and now I'm here thinking about shit." I play with the screw in my hand.

"I'll be there in a minute." Candice hangs up.

The screw that's bothering me is attached to a cabinet I asked Knox to fix over three months ago. He's usually so good about doing the things I ask. There are also cracks in the windowsill. Knox and I aren't the only fractured thing in this house.

I hear Candice open the door, and I look up to see a car I don't recognize in the driveway. "Did Mick buy you a car?" I ask as she enters the kitchen.

"No. I borrowed his." She sits at the table, and I join her.

"Ah, I see." I gaze out into the backyard.

"Are you all right, love?" she asks.

"No, I'm not," I say and look back at her.

"What happened?"

"Knox lied."

"About?"

"The nanny. Apparently, she kissed him." I fidget with the mug in front of me.

"I'm guessing the kiss isn't what's really bothering you?" she asks.

I take a long sip from my coffee cup; the coffee is freezing now.

"No, it's the lie," I say.

"I don't understand why he'd lie about it. It doesn't make sense. People come on to him all the time, and he always tells you. Hell, I've always been jealous by how close you two are."

"I guess we're not doing so great these days."

"Is there something going on? With him?"

"If you mean drugs or alcohol, no. I think he's going through shit. When he was in New York, he was talking about quitting The Hestons. It doesn't seem to be making him happy anymore. And now, with the pressure of finishing the album. I don't know. I can't keep making excuses for your brother no matter how much I love him." I let out a sob.

"Fair." She places a hand over mine and gives it a squeeze.

"It sucks. I needed him to be a comfort to me for the next couple of days. I don't know what I'm going to do. I've put up with so much and for Knox to lie about something so small makes me feel crazy. Like what else could he be hiding, you know?" I say.

Except I know what he's hiding. And that could be a silent killer all on its own. The thought of losing Knox terrifies me.

"Yes," she whispers.

"I'm sorry. I shouldn't be unloading all of this on you. He's your brother." I shake my head as silent tears stream down my face.

"He may be my brother, but you're my best friend."

"Thank you." I give her a small smile.

"So, I'm scared to ask, but what are you going to do?" she asks.

"I don't know." I hesitate. "I think we might need to take a break."

"No." She gasps.

"I think the stress of everything going on with The Talons, now Brandon, and Knox not knowing what he wants right now—it might be for the best if he takes some time for himself to figure it out. I'm going to take Lottie with us on tour. He needs to clear his head. He needs to decide what he wants." I wipe the tears rolling down my cheeks.

"If you're sure," she says.

"I am. It'll be all right. No matter what he decides, we'll all be all right." I'm not sure if I'm trying to convince her or me. I've never felt pain like this.

"What did he say when you told him?" she asks.

"I haven't yet."

I want her to convince me to stay and fight for him. I want her to tell me everything is going to be all right, even if it's only to make me feel better. I'm so tired of being the strong one.

"Oh. What's going on with Brandon?"

I pause. I'm grateful for the topic change. "His girlfriend, Hannah, has been diagnosed with breast cancer, and it doesn't look good."

Brandon had called me a bit earlier to tell me he can't come back. He's not sure how long Hannah has left, and he wants to be with her.

She gulps. "No—that's heartbreaking. Is he okay?"

"He's not. He's not coming back with us to resume the tour."

"I need to tell him I'm thinking of him." She says and stands. "Knox loves you too, you know."

"I know. I'm just wondering if love is enough. Is it really going to outweigh everything else?" I ask.

"I don't know, but I sure hope so," she says.

"Me too," I whisper.

18

KNOX

Mick's late. I could really use the distraction. With Caroline kicking me out, my mind can't really process anything else. Not only that, but Lena also called again about the album. I need everything to fucking stop. I need to deal with my shit, not have everything get incredibly worse.

"Hey," Mick says as he gets inside. He smells of cigarettes. Good to know he stopped for a smoke before he came in.

"Oh, hey," he says. I've been crying on and off the entire afternoon. I'm sure I look a state right now.

"You all right, mate?" he asks.

"Yup," he says. I'm not getting into my emotional baggage with Mick fuckin' Davies.

"Are you sure?" he asks.

"Uh." I hesitate.

Give Mick a chance. He might surprise you. Rex's words echo through my mind.

"You don't have to tell me." Mick shrugs and takes a seat.

"God, I wish I could be high right now." I play with the pencil in my hand. Emotions are so much easier to deal with when you're on cocaine.

"You are not allowed. I'm not getting murdered by Caroline or Candice," Mick says.

"I doubt Caroline would care right now." The words tumble out before I can stop them.

"Ah, so it's girl troubles then." Mick nods.

"I'm an idiot." I let out a breath.

"What happened?" He asks.

"Caroline said that we're done unless I get my shit together. Our nanny kissed me, and I lied about it. I also don't know what I'm doing anymore. Am I making a mistake wanting to quit music, or is it the right path for me?"

Looking over at Mick, it's clear he hasn't heard a single thing I've said. So much for opening up to me.

"Mick?" I interrupt his thoughts.

"Sorry." He shakes his head. "Can you say that again?"

"It's all right. You don't need to hear my problems."

"Don't be a chick. Tell me again."

"Our nanny kissed me, and I didn't tell Caroline. Then my mother let it slip."

"Always tell your girl, mate." Mick chuckles.

"I know. I don't know why I didn't."

"I do."

"Oh, do you?" he raises an eyebrow at me.

"You liked it, and you're ashamed."

My jaw drops. There are moments in the self-deprecation that I've felt unwanted, and it did feel nice to have someone throw themselves at me. "How did you know? I pushed her away, but a part of me missed being wanted."

"Your wife wants you. So does your little lass," he says.

"I know, but being apart and going through all of this weird shit in my head and with the band, I don't know what the hell came over me." I hang my head. I sound like such a loser.

"It's hard, I think, being away from what you know—being away from the one thing that gets you through the day. The one thing that you know better than yourself and knows you better than you know yourself," he says.

My mind is ignited, and I grab my pen and journal. "That's brilliant."

"What?" Mick frowns.

"You gave me an idea," I say.

"I want writing credits." He grins.

"Of course," I say.

We write for a couple of hours before we have a good working song.

"I think if you hit the endnote of this line just a little higher, it'd work brilliantly," Mick says to me.

"Yes, you're so right." I nod.

"We're done." He smiles.

"Shall we record?" I ask.

"Can we get to this tomorrow?" he asks.

"Sure. No problem," I say. Except I'm disappointed. I don't want to be alone right now. Even Mick's company is welcome.

"You should go home too."

"I know. You're right." I sigh. It's almost midnight.

"She loves you."

"But is love enough anymore?"

"Fingers crossed." Mick gives me a nod before he leaves.

I take a few more moments before I decide it's time to go home. I need to make this better.

"Caroline?" I whisper through the dark. Guessing by the tissues beside the bed, she's been crying most of the night.

My parents and Lottie are both in their rooms.

"What?" she asks.

"Can we talk, please?"

She sits up and turns on the lamp situated on the bedside table. I sit beside her, and all I want to do is hold her. She's always been the shoulder for me to cry on, and it's wrecking her that we're struggling through something else.

"I'm sorry," I say. She looks at me, and her eyes are puffy and bloodshot.

"I know." She crosses her arms around her torso.

"I didn't tell you because I didn't know how to say it. Not only about the nanny but also about the depression. I haven't felt like myself for so long, and then when you left, it became more noticeable."

"Knox, I forgive you," she says.

"You do?" My heart swells.

"Yes."

"Caroline, you're the most amazing woman." I wrap my arms around her, but she doesn't hug me back.

"I don't think you're going to think that in a few minutes." She sighs, and I drop my arms.

"What? Why?" he asks.

"We need a break. I need a break more specifically," she says.

"You're leaving me?" My throat goes dry.

"No, I just- I don't know—

"What the fuck are you saying?" I'm angry.

"We need time apart to think about what we're doing. We're not us right now. I want to be us. I'm not saying I want to see other people; I think we need a break to re-evaluate what we truly want and out of life, what we want out of each other. I don't trust you, Knox. I've watched you go throu—"

"That was then! This is now! What are you doing to us, Caroline? If you want me out of your life, then I'll go, but I love you. Please don't do this." I'm begging. She can't leave me.

"I have a daughter to worry about this time. If you lie about something like this, what will happen if you relapse. What if you have Lottie and something happens?" I ask.

"You're not being fair. All of this because of what? Depression?" He runs a hand through his hair.

"No. It's the lying. You haven't been honest with me. You haven't been honest with yourself either." Her voice wobbles, and tears spill down her cheeks.

"I love you, Caroline. There is nothing in this world that's going to change that. There is nothing in this world that would ever let me put Lottie in harm's way. I have never given a shit about anything as much as you two. So don't do this," I say. I'm desperate.

"I'm going to stay at a hotel for the next day before I fly back to the States. I'm going to come get Lottie tomorrow. She's coming out on the road with me. When I get back from Canada, we can talk about this."

"That's two months away!"

"I think we need this time."

"Don't do this. I'm begging you. Please." I kneel before her and lay my head in her lap. I'm fully crying now. I want her to stay. The pain is unbearable.

"Knox, I'm sorry." Caroline is crying as hard as me now.

"What does this mean?" I look up at her.

"It means we're going to sort some things out. Figure out if this relationship is still working for both of us. Figure out if love really is enough," she says.

"I'm not going to stop loving you. I'm going to wait till you come to your senses," I sit up and wipe my eyes.

"I don't want you to stop loving me. I'm not going to stop loving you, Knox. I need some time to get my head on straight. You do too. Focus on your music. Focus on the tour. Focus on anything but me. I'll make sure Lottie FaceTimes with you any time you want," she says.

"Fine." I'm defeated as she gets out of bed and starts throwing things into her weekender. I'm helpless. Before she goes to leave our room, I call out to her. "I love you."

"I love you too," she says but doesn't turn around.

She shuts the door, and I'm left alone in our bedroom. I curl up into a ball and cry. I've lost everything.

19

CAROLINE

I can't lose my nerve. We need this. We need a break. The tears pour down my cheeks, and my shoulders start to shake as I walk down the stairs. I get to the kitchen and take a deep breath.

"Caroline?" Alan says from behind me. "You all right?"

"I'm fine." I wipe my eyes.

"You're crying?" he says it as more of a question than a statement. Alan and I have always been close. I knew when I met him; he was the kind of father I had always wanted. Knox's parents and Candice were the only other people who had gone through all the same things as me.

"I'm leaving."

Alan opens his arms and motions for me to hug him. I do as I'm told and feel some comfort as he wraps his arms around me. After a minute of him holding me, I pull back.

"He loves you," Alan says, "I've never seen him love anything as much as he loves you. Not even music." Alan sits at the kitchen table and motions for me to join him.

"I know that. And I love him too, but I can't keep wondering when the next time he'll lie to me is. What if he relapses? I can't go through that again." I cry harder.

"Me either. I'm sure my heart would give out. So what are you going to do? Are you two separating?" he asks.

"No. Well. I don't know. I need a break. I need to focus on something other than Knox. He needs to figure out what he wants too," I say.

"I know he does." Alan nods. "He's going through something. I think you're doing the right thing. Giving him space to figure it out."

"You do?" I ask.

"I do. You're a smart lass. We knew when Knox brought you home that there was something special about you. And we were so happy when he realized that too. You are everything that made him smarten up. If you believe anything, believe that. And Cynthia and I will always be grateful to you. For the rest of our lives. But you have always been so careful taking care of everyone else that you haven't had the time to take care of yourself. I think you should let Lottie come stay with us. You both need to focus on yourselves," he says. I look at him.

"Yeah, I agree," I say. I know he's right. Lottie needs to be with people who are consistent for a while. He stands up, and I stand too.

"We love you, Caroline. That will never change. No matter what." He gives me a tight squeeze before he walks out of the kitchen. I pick up my bag and head out of my house. This is what's for the best.

I wake up in the morning with the sun streaming in. Brandon texts me to ask if we can meet at a café close to his house. I walk in and see him sitting at a booth at the back of the restaurant.

"Hi, B," I say. He stands and gives me a quick hug before we sit. I notice people are starting to stare at us.

"How are you?" he asks.

"I'm okay."

"You don't look all right."

"Why are we talking about me? We should be talking about you."

"I would love to talk about anything but me. Is everything good at home?" he asks.

"Not exactly." I look down. I slide my sunglasses down over my face. The tears start to spill down my cheeks again.

"Don't cry. There are too many people here," Brandon whispers.

"I'll try. We are on a break, I guess. We're taking some time," I say.

"I'm sorry." Brandon pats my hand.

"Thanks." I give him a half-hearted smile.

"What about Lottie?" he asks.

"She is going to stay with Knox's parents for a while. Take a break and be a kid for a bit," I say.

"The rumours are going to run rampant," he says.

"I know." I nod. "How are you?"

"I'm not good. The cancer is bad. It is the worst-case scenario. We're lucky if we get a month together." He rubs his temples.

"I'm so sorry." I get out of the booth and sit on his side. I wrap an arm around him.

"The lads are going to be so mad."

"Don't worry about that. They'll understand. Take all the time you need."

"Thanks, Caroline."

We sit in the booth for an hour before we go our separate ways. I need to go back to the States.

I get to the hotel and start to pack my bag again. My phone rings, and I see Candice's name appear on the screen.

"Hey. See you guys soon?" I ask.

Candice is crying so hard I don't understand what she's saying.

"Whoa, whoa. Slow down. What happened?" I ask. My heart seizes, and for a second, I'm wondering if Knox has relapsed for real this time.

"M—Mick. He fuckin' lied. He and Tommy—" she bawls harder. I'm instantly relieved, then guilt takes over. Candice is clearly devastated, and I'm just thinking about myself.

"Take a breath." I mimic breathing techniques, and I hear her take a deep inhale. "Now, what happened?"

"It was all a bet, Caroline. Mick made a bet with Tommy that he could sleep with me. It was all to get back at Knox." She sobs after she finishes her sentence. I take a seat on my bed.

"Oh, Candice." *That fucker.* I knew he was up to something. I thought he loved her, though. Scratch that. I know he loves her.

"It was all some joke." She sniffs.

"I don't believe it all was a joke. I do think he loves you," I say.

"He doesn't," she says.

I don't argue with her. She's broken in half. She loves him more than I've seen her love anyone.

"I have to quit the tour," she says.

No. I've lost Brandon, and now Candice is quitting. I've lost all my comfort in one swoop.

"Are you sure?" I ask even though I know she can't come back.

"Yes. I'm going to stay in London. I'm sorry, Car."

"Don't apologize. Take care of yourself. I have to finish packing and go to the airport. I'm so sorry, Candice," I say.

"I'll be all right. Going to go to your place and getting my parents to take care of me for a bit." She lets out a sigh.

"That makes sense. Love you, Candy."

"You too." She hangs up.

Mick isn't at the airport. I text him, and he replies instantly, saying he and Tommy aren't coming back today. I didn't even know Tommy was in London. Everything is fucked. The flight back to Chicago is long. Thankfully, I got to take the private plane back so I could hide from the prying eyes of other people. It isn't enough that I'm taking a break from my husband. I also have to do it in front of billions of people. I get to the hotel in Chicago and check-in. I call Rick and get him to meet me in my room.

"Hi, beautiful. How was the trip?" he asks after I let him in. He sits on the chair in my room, and I sit across from him.

"Exhausting."

"I bet. You had such a quick trip."

"Yeah, I know. Faster than I had expected."

"So, is Brandon coming back tomorrow then?"

"Brandon needs time off." I sigh.

"I figured but wasn't sure. Hannah's cancer is bad then?" he asks.

I swallow hard. "She has maybe a month."

"Well, we can find a replacement or something." He strokes his chin.

"There's something else," I say, and he raises his eyebrows. "Candice quit. Tommy and Mick didn't come back with me either. He didn't give me a timeframe of when they are coming back.

"What?" Rick looks like he's going to pass out. "When did Tommy go to London?"

"I have no idea. I was going to ask you the same thing," I say.

"We're postponing until further notice." He shakes his head. "We can't continue a tour with Conner and Kane—who the hell even knows where those two are!"

"There's more," I say.

"Caroline, I don't think I can take any more."

"It's nothing too major. Knox and I are taking a break. Lottie's going with his parents for a while. We're trying to figure ourselves out."

"That's pretty major. I'm so sorry." He pats my knee.

"I think I'm going to stay in Chicago for a couple of days anyway. Need a bit of a breather," I say.

"Sounds good. I'm sorry to cut this short, but I have to go sort everything out." He stands, and I nod.

"I'll cancel the venues and chat with the crew."

"Thanks." He gives a smile before he disappears out the door.

Five days go by fast when you're running off your feet the entire time. Knox and I haven't spoken other than a few texts. Lottie is having a great time in Belfast. Everything is seemingly getting back to normal in the most abnormal time.

My phone buzzes, and it's a text from Rick letting me know he's heading back to the UK this afternoon. I have a flight back booked in a couple of days.

I dial Candice's number. "Hey, love. How's Belfast?"

"Oh, good. Lottie and mum popped round to the shop. I'm reading a book for the first time in forever. Also, guess what?" Her tone is the happiest it's been over the last few days.

"What?"

"I think I have a job in a salon in London!"

"Ah, that's amazing." I smile.

"I'm not going to let this drag me down. I need to get back on my feet," she says.

"I'm so proud of you. I'm heading home in a couple of days. We officially cancelled the tour. The announcement goes out tomorrow." I sigh. While a part of me is relieved, the other part is going to miss this tour.

"Have you talked to Mick?" she asks.

Mick had texted me a few times, trying to get Candice's whereabouts, telling me how much he fucked up and how much he loves Candice. I believe him, but it's not my decision to make.

"I believe he's still in London. There were talks that he was going to take Violet on a trip, but I'm not sure," I say.

"Right, of course." She pauses. "Caroline, I know you don't want to hear this, but I'm worried about Knox. All he did was go back and forth from the studio to your house. He didn't want to talk to anyone. He's cancelled the tour, so I don't know what his plans are."

"What? He what?" I couldn't breathe. Knox had cancelled the tour. "I don't understand. I told him to go. Did he give a reason?"

"No. He got Lena and the label to release a statement saying that the tour is postponed until further notice," she says. "I think things are bad with the album. He's finished it, but it sounds like the label doesn't love it."

"Shit, that's not good. He's worked so hard on it. How are things with him and Felix?"

"Better. Felix has been spending a lot of time with him. I think once Felix and I spoke to Knox together, it simmered his anger down."

"Good. He needs his best friend, even if he is a douchebag."

She's silent, and I can tell she's holding back.

"What?" I ask.

"It's just—you should call him," she says.

"I can't," I say.

"He'd love to hear from you," she says.

"I've texted him, and he hasn't called me either." I sound like a child.

"I know. I get it. Hey, I've got to go. I'll get Lottie to give you a call when she's back, okay?"

"Sounds great. Thanks," I say.

"Later, Car!" She clicks off.

I should call him. He is my husband, after all. I pull out my phone and type out a message.

Me: *Heard about the tour. Hope you're OK. xx*

I place my phone down and stare at it—willing him to reply. I miss him more than I want to say.

Knox replies within a second.

Knox: *Thanks. Needed the break to figure out some things. I miss you more than anything. Xx*

Me: *Same.*

He doesn't text me back, and I'm grateful. I'm going to take the next few days to relax and then figure everything else out when I get back to London.

20

KNOX

"I know I fucked up." Mick is pacing back and forth at the studio. It's been a week since Candice broke up with him, and he's been here every day. Thankfully he and Felix have excellent timing and keep missing each other. Mick has helped me finish the album, even though the label still isn't sure if they're going to release it. Apparently, it's a bit darker than my other stuff. *No shit.*

"I'm not giving you my Ma and Da's address. Listen, I'm mad as fuck at you but really, who am I to judge anymore? We're both pretty pathetic." I lace my fingers together and put them behind my head.

"You know I love her. I was a prick. I'm not denying that. But I am not the same man who started dating your sister. She's made me better." He slumps into the chair next to me and kicks his feet up on the coffee table.

I believe him. I believe him because I've been there.

"Now that we're both off indefinitely, do you think we're going to become best mates?" Mick smirks at me.

"Never in a million years." I laugh. The truth is, though, the more time we spend together, the more I like the fucker. With Lottie and Caroline both away, it's nice to have the company. I'm lost in my thoughts, and I look up to see Mick staring at me.

"What? Sorry," I say.

"I said, are you going to see Caroline when she's back tomorrow?" he asks.

"Caroline is back tomorrow?" It's hard to swallow. She didn't tell me she was coming back. Sure, I knew it had to be soon, but I figured we'd have everything worked out, and she'd come home.

"She didn't tell you?" Mick asks.

"No. I'm surprised she told you," I say.

"Oh, she didn't. She told Brandon, who told me." He shrugs.

"How's he doing?" I ask.

"He's been at the hospice mostly. She's fading quick. I feel so bad for him."

"Same. And for Hannah and her family. It's all so sad. And here we are, a couple of idiot blokes who can't fucking get their shit together."

"Two incredibly huge idiots."

I turn, and my wife is standing in the doorway.

"Way to pull the old surprise." Mick smiles and stands up.

"Good to see you too." She laughs and hugs him. She then hits him upside the head. "That's for messing shit up with Candice. You really screwed up."

"Thanks for that. I will make it up to her. You guys will be my family officially. I swear to you." He pats me on the back.

"Don't threaten us." I tease.

"I'll leave you two. Good to see you, Caroline." He gives me a nod.

"You too, actually," she says.

Mick leaves, and an awkward silence hangs between Caroline and me.

"Who knew we'd end up friends with him?" Caroline gives me a tight smile.

"Definitely not me." I shake my head. She comes into the room more and sits where Mick vacated.

"It's good to see you." I don't move to touch her. I'm scared she's like a deer, and she'll bolt if I make any sudden movements.

"You too. I know I'm breaking the needing space rule," she says.

"I didn't ever want that rule," I remind her.

"Me either. I felt like I had no choice." She sighs.

I reach out for her hand, and she lets me take it. "What are you feeling now?"

"Like I want to be with you. That a week without talking to you or FaceTiming with you is too long, even when I was in New York, it didn't feel so bad because I knew we were good." Her eyes look into mine.

"Same. Except I couldn't even get through a week without you, period. I've been a wreck." I squeeze her hand.

"How did we get here? When we were younger, it all felt easier, you know?" she sighs.

I nod. "It did seem easier. Or maybe we just forget now because everything in the past is so distant."

"Yeah, you're probably right." She places her other hand on top of mine. "How are you feeling?"

"Not great, but not worse? I started seeing this psychiatrist—Dr. Dergousoff. She's great. She's prescribed me some anti-depressants, but they take a bit to kick in. They also give me headaches which she says is normal. I have to push through this stage," I say.

Caroline starts to tear up.

"Hey. What's wrong?" I ask.

"I should have been here. I shouldn't have left you when you needed me most." She sobs.

"Listen to me, baby girl. You need to stop worrying about me and take care of yourself too. Yes, I'm going through something, but I also need to take a bit of responsibility for myself. We learned that with rehab. It doesn't matter how much I love you. It had to be in me to get clean. This is like that in a way." I pull her close to me, and she rests her head on my chest.

"That makes sense." She sniffs and doesn't move.

I take a deep inhale. She smells like her shampoo, honey and vanilla. "I'm not going to tour anymore. I've talked to Felix and Danny. I'm going to be your road husband. I'll take care of Lottie and help out with stuff on whatever tour you work on. I can write music and produce tracks when we're in London."

She sits up. "You're serious?"

"Deadly." I smile, and she throws herself back into me.

"I love you so much. Let's never do this again."

"I love you, and I agree." I laugh, and she kisses me.

Our kisses become desperate as she climbs on top of me. She slides her shirt over her head, and her lacy pink bra makes me hard instantly.

"Have I mentioned how much I've missed you?" I grin, and she slaps me playfully.

"The feeling is very mutual. Now fuck me, Mr. Bryan," she says.

That's all the encouragement I need. I pick her up and put her on her feet so I can strip off her jeans. I pull down the matching lacy pink panties, and our lips crash together again. I gently push her back down to the couch and pull my shirt over my head. I kneel in front of her and part her legs gently. I leave kisses all up and down both of her thighs.

"You're going to tease me?" She asks.

"Only a little." I wink. I make my way up to her core and run my tongue from top to bottom. She shivers and closes her eyes. She tastes so fucking good. She's wet already, and it's driving me crazy. But this is about her. I want to make her come before I bury myself deep inside her.

My fingers move up and down her slit until I slip a finger inside. She lets out a moan, making my erection more painful. I use my tongue to tease her clit while my fingers pump inside of her. It only takes a few moments of constant motion for her to start pulsating around me.

Her legs are shaking as she grips the back of my hair with both of her hands. She grinds against my tongue and fingers. "Knox!"

Her release is sweet, and we make eye contact as she comes back down to earth.

"God, I've missed this." She breathes, still panting.

"Me too, baby." I stand and unbutton my jeans. I pull my boxer briefs off at the same time.

Caroline licks her lips, and there's nothing more beautiful. Our mouths crash into each other again. My tip is sliding up and down her folds, and she starts to moan again. I flick her nipple while my other hand grips her hips. Before I enter her, I press my erection against her core, making her gasp.

"This is what you do to me, Caroline. No one else makes me feel the way you do, and no one else will. I love you. I love you more than anything in the entire world." I kiss her, and she smiles.

"I love you too." She kisses me again before tangling her hands in my hair. I move my mouth down to one of her nipples. I bite and suck on it. Caroline's grasp tightens on my hair. I need to be inside her now.

She lifts her hips, and I guide myself into her, filling her. My hips touch against hers, and I rock against her. My tip must have found that perfect spot because Caroline exhales as her eyes roll into the back of her head. *Jackpot.*

"Please don't stop." She begs as her hands move down to grip my ass.

Our lips find each other again, and I pull my hips back, slamming them back into her. She digs her nails into me, and I moan into her mouth. I'm already ready to fall apart. My hips start to move faster. My thrusts are getting harder. I bite down on her neck.

"Yes, Knox. Fuck. Yes." She's panting again as she tightens around me.

"I want you to come for me, Caroline." My teeth nip her ear, and her moans grow louder.

"Knox." She breathes out my name. "Don't stop."

She squeezes me tighter as I pump harder and harder until she's calling out my name over and over again. I jerk to a stop, letting out a sound from deep within my throat. I'm still on top of her, not wanting this moment to end. We're both breathing heavy, trying to get our control back. Her heart is pounding in her chest, which is pressed to mine.

"See, we can never break up. There's no one in this world who's this good in bed." Caroline giggles.

"It's a good thing I love you, Caroline Harper-Bryan. And damn, do I love you more than anything." I lean back so I can look into her eyes.

"I love you too, Knox. So much." She smiles.

This is my happily ever after, and damn, there's nothing better.

EPILOGUE

CAROLINE

ONE YEAR LATER

"Candice! You're going to be late." I call her, but I don't hear any movement.

"Maybe I should go get her?" Conner asks. He's in a navy-blue suit and a white button-up shirt underneath. I curse myself for thinking it, but he looks so handsome. I'm not the only one who thinks so. Violet is standing in her navy-blue dress, staring at him, totally oblivious to anything else.

"No, let's give her one more moment," I sigh.

"We're going to be late," Knox mumbles from beside me.

"It's fine. It'll be fine," I say and straighten his tie. "Lottie, you look gorgeous."

My daughter is standing next to her dad in a poofy dress. Her hair is done up to the side, but you can see the curls the hairdresser put in before making it an updo.

"I'm coming. I'm coming." Candice finally emerges at the top of the stairs. Her wedding dress is a perfect silhouette that clings to her body. It's an off-white lace gown, and on her train is beautiful beading. She's not wearing a veil, choosing to let her curls hang loose. She looks like a princess.

Tears well in my eyes. "You look—"

"Caroline, don't cry. If you cry, then I'm going to cry, and I paid too much for my make-up to ruin it before pictures." She laughs.

"Sorry. It must be the hormones." I let out a small chuckle. I look down at my growing belly. Six months pregnant. I had asked Candice to wait to get married till after I had the baby, but Mick said he wasn't going to wait longer than a year to marry her.

"I cannot believe you're pregnant," Candice says. "I can't believe I'm getting married. To Mick Davies."

"Prick." We both say at the same time and laugh.

"Sorry, Vi," Candice says.

Violet shrugs. "I'm used to it. And he really was."

"So, as your man of honour, do I get to walk down the aisle first?" Conner asks.

"Conner, you're not the man of honour. You're just a bride's man. Caroline is the maid of honour." Candice shakes her head.

"If there's going to be a man of honour, may I throw my hat into the ring?" Knox asks.

"Hey, you two! Stop trying to take my job," I say.

"Okay. The music is playing. Everyone line up! Lottie, you go before your mom. It goes Violet, Conner, Knox, Lottie, Caroline, then me and Da. Wait—" Candice stops. "Where's Da?"

"Right here." We turn to see Alan in a suit that matches Knox and Conner's.

"All right. You can go now, Vi. I'm ready." Candice smiles.

We all make our way down the aisle without a hitch. Brandon is standing next to Mick as his best man. Tommy seemed a bit hurt by the decision but ultimately was fine when Brandon said he could plan the bachelor party. Brandon's grown a long beard, and even though I know he's happy to be here, there's a lot hidden beneath the surface. The Talons are set to go out on tour again in the new year and there's still a lot up in the air on whether Brandon is going to come or not. Next to him is Tommy. Tommy waves into the crowd at Nadine and their infant daughter Royal. They're not together, but I'm impressed with how well they're co-parenting. Next to him is Kane. Loveable, steady, and always calm Kane. His wife Charity is sitting next to Nadine. I forgot that they know each other. Rex rounds out Mick's groomsmen, and that's not a surprise. Rex has also been tearing up the entire day. Maybe Mick's parents aren't great, but he and Violet are lucky to have Rex.

The couple says their vows. Everyone cheers, and it's time to dance. Candice and Mick decided to get married in Belfast in an old castle that Candice had been dreaming of since she was a kid. Everything had turned out gorgeous. The best part is the ocean view from the castle.

I stand close to the edge and stare out at the ocean. What a difference a year makes.

"Can you believe we're here?" Knox comes up behind me and wraps his arm around my waist.

"Honestly? No. If you told me Candice was going to be Candice Davies back then, I would have died from laughter." I chuckle.

"I know. It's crazy." Knox shakes his head.

I lean my head against his shoulder and rest my hands on my stomach. The baby gives me a big kick. "Oh."

"What?" Knox asks.

"Nothing, just a few kicks." I smile.

"My son is already acting up. I told you a boy is going to inherit my unruliness." Knox laughs.

"I wouldn't have him any other way." I tilt my head, and Knox kisses me.

He bends down so he can talk to my belly. "Now, Henry, give your mom a break. She's going to have to keep us both in line now. She deserves a few more months of rest."

I laugh and run a hand through his hair. "I hope he gets your curls, like Lottie."

"I hope he gets your personality. Then we'll know he's going to basically be perfect." He kisses me again.

"He's going to be perfect no matter what because he's ours," I say.

"True." Knox nods and wraps his arm back around my waist.

I lean my head against his shoulder again, and he rests his head on top of mine. This life might not be a fairy tale, but it's mine, and I'm so happy for that.

The End

Losing Hannah is the worst thing that happened to Brandon. Now it's two years later, and she's still in his heart. Escaping to Italy seemed like the best idea, and now Brooke has him wondering if maybe he can love again.

Flip the page for a preview of Healing The Rock Star's Heart Coming to your shelves November 23, 2021.

HEALING THE ROCK STAR'S HEART
CHAPTER 1
BROOKE

There's a loud clatter from behind me, but my eyes are trained on the man in front of me. "What do you mean you're married?"

"I got married last month." His thick Italian accent is still as smooth as the first time I heard it two years ago.

"But I thought…" I close my mouth and meet Angelo's gaze again. I, Brooke Collins, have been so sure that he's the love of my life. Two years ago, Angelo told me that I was his one true love, and now here he was married, married to some other woman who probably has matching chocolate brown eyes and hair as dark as night. Thank God this café has alcohol.

"I'm sorry, Brookie," he says. He's called me Brookie since the day we met in this exact café.

"You need a vacation," my best friend, Jessie, says as she looks over at me.

"I do not. I'm—fine," I say.

"No, you're not fine. You and Liam broke up five months ago, and your apartment still looks like a shrine to him." She sighs.

"We were together for four years and lived together" The walls of my apartment are full of pictures of us.

"I know that, darling, but you need to go. Get away from Seattle for a while." Her eyes are sympathetic, which made a sad situation a bit worse.

"What happens if I leave, and Liam wants to get back together?" I ask.

"Has that happened yet?" she asks.

"Well, not exactly..." I say.

"Sleeping together once in a while doesn't mean you're getting back together."

"I know. But I'm not sure if going all the way to Italy is the answer." I cross my arms. There are still a few boxes with Liam's stuff. He's coming to get it in a few days.

"It's definitely the answer. All you have to do is buy a ticket, and seeing as how you're the best saver I know, you for sure have the cash to spare."

"What about—"

"No. School is out for the summer. You have no excuse not to go. I don't want to have paid for the month for no reason," Jessie says. Jessie has paid for a month's rent for an apartment in Amalfi Town before getting engaged to her boyfriend. Now she wants to spend the summer with his family in England.

"You are supposed to go and write in Italy. That is your dream, remember?"

"It was my dream, but now this is my path."

"Fine. I'll go. I mean, what have I got to lose anymore?"

In the days leading up to the flight, I had everything in order. From the second the bus had pulled up to the Amalfi Coast, I had fallen in love. Everything was bright and colourful, loud Italian's hand talking everywhere, and the salty sea smell hit me when I stepped onto the street. It was perfect.

"Don't be sorry," I say to Angelo. It's crazy of me to think that someone like him wouldn't get snapped up in the two years I've spent away from Amalfi. The only thing was now I'm here permanently. It had taken all my courage to apply for a job teaching English in Amalfi, but I figured it would be worth it. I could recreate the magic I had found in this place the first time, but after only being here six hours, it's obvious I've misjudged everything.

"Brooke, you are still so beautiful. Your hair is still as curly as the day you left." Angelo smiles. I run a hand through my hair. My hair is brown, but my eyes are blue, and I have a pale complexion, which makes me stand out in Italy.

"Thank you. You're beautiful too." I blurt, and he is. He is the hottest man that I have ever seen. Even when I thought that Liam was good-looking, he's still nowhere near Angelo's God-like physique and stature.

"Grazie." He chuckles.

"I still can't believe you're married." I look down at his tanned left hand and see a gold band gracing his third finger. I'm not sure how I missed that.

"Gabriella is wonderful. You would like her," he says and smiles. He loves her.

"I'm sure I would." I smile. I look past him at the counter of the café. Looking around this place, it hasn't changed one bit.

My first night in Amalfi was all sleep. I unpacked my things in my one-bedroom apartment and stared off the deck at the water. Jessie picked an amazing place. The following day, I decide to head down to a café that I had seen at the end of the block. Coffee fills my nostrils. It's amazing.

"Ciao," the barista greets me.

"Ciao... uhm uno espresso per favore?" I say in the little Italian I learned before I left.

"Si."

"Uno croissant?" I say, pointing at the chocolate croissant in the case beside me.

"Si." She nods.

"Grazie," I say as she hands me the croissant and coffee.

"Preggo," she says.

I find a seat next to the window and take a deep breath. I'm in Italy.

"Bongiorno," I hear and look up into dark brown eyes

"Hi," I say.

"American?" he asks.

"Si." I blush.

"I am Angelo." He takes a seat across from me.

"Brooke," I'm staring at a figment of my imagination. I have to be.

"Brookie." His accent is charming me already. "Why are you in Amalfi?"

"Adventure," I whisper.

"If adventure is what you seek, then come with me," he says.

"I don't know you." I come back to Earth. We're not in some romance novel where this works out. I might get kidnapped!

"I own a..." He stops to search for the English word. "Boat company. Tours. I can show you." The café is located across from the marina.

"Okay." I down my shot of espresso. I text Jessie quick, in case this guy does turn out to be a weirdo. She can track me on Find My Friends.

"Come. I promise fun." He smiles. "I will give you your adventure Brookie."

"I sure hope so." I take his outstretched hand, and we intertwine our fingers.

"How long are you here?" Angelo asks.

"What?" I say. I can't tell him the mortifying truth. The fact that I'm stuck here for the next year at least.

"How long are you here for?" he asks again.

"Oh uh—for a while," I say.

"A while?" His eyebrows scrunch together.

"Long time?" I say.

"Ah," he says. An awkwardness falls between us. Maybe he's secretly hoping I'm joking.

"Do you remember that night we spent in Ravello?" I cut the silence.

"Si," he says as slowly as anyone could say a one-syllable word.

"What was that hotel called?" I ask. I don't know why I want to reminisce. It's not going to somehow transport us back in time, and he's not married.

"Brookie, I never meant to hurt you," he says.

"But you did."

"You have been gone a long time." He takes a sip from the red wine in front of him.

"You never once mentioned a girlfriend in your letters."

"I'm sorry."

"No problem." I want this conversation to end. Dear God, do I want to be anywhere but here.

"It's a problem," he says.

"Why?" I ask.

"Why?" He frowns. The worst part is that we could be having this conversation in Italian because I learned it for him. But I can't tell him that humiliating detail now.

"Why is it a problem?" I say.

"I care for you."

"Right."

"Remember Pantone?" he asks. *How could I forget?* He had told me he loved me while we sat out looking at the stars. We had hiked up from Amalfi Town, and we had laughed the entire way.

"I remember." I nod.

"What I say then was true. I love you, but Brookie, I am not in love with you," he says.

Ouch.

"Got it. Well, thanks for meeting me." Now I really need him to go. I need a drink stronger than the wine. When I found him on the docks earlier today to ask him to meet up, I had no idea of the pain that would come with it. I had rushed into his arms, and we had embraced for so long that everything felt right. I had missed the wedding ring then too.

"Brookie, if you need anything…" he trails off.

"I'll be great. Thanks," I give him a small smile.

"Call me if you have any problems," he says before getting up to leave.

"Sure. Thanks, Angelo." I watch the back of the man I loved walk away for good. The last time this happened, two years ago, Angelo had cried and told me that he would wait for me.

"Wow, that was harsh." A deep voice causes me to look up.

My gaze meets another set of brown eyes, except his are more hazel. He's handsome, but a bushy beard covers most of his face.

"Excuse me?" I glare.

"That sounded like it sucked," he says in a British accent.

"Did you listen to the entire thing?" I ask.

"Yeah, I did." He doesn't break eye contact with me.

"Awesome." Heat creeps into my cheeks. The rest of the room is filled with couples who are smiling and holding hands. This guy and I are now the only two people who are sitting alone.

"You were getting broken up with, in public—it was hard not to listen." He shrugs.

"You're an ass," I say.

"I'm sorry. Can I buy you a drink?" He stands.

"Unreal! I am not in the mood to be hit on.

"I'm not hitting on you." He chuckles.

"You're not?" The embarrassment is back.

"No, I'm not. Not after how it seems that you make life-changing decisions on short encounters." He pulls the chair out where Angelo had vacated and sits across from me.

"It wasn't that short."

"How long were you and Raphael together?" He motions for the server and orders us both a scotch neat. I'm not usually a scotch drinker, but a little burn to distract me from my breaking heart is a welcome change.

"Angelo," I say. "And a month."

"A month two years ago?" He had listened to every word. Screw Angelo, and his inability to tell me earlier.

"Yes," I admit.

"And now you live here? Or at least that's what it sounds like to me."

"I..." There's nothing else I can say but the truth. "Yes."

"That guy must have been some shag." He laughs.

"That's not all it was. That guy showed me things that no one has—not just sex." The server places our drinks down, and I take a sip. Scotch is the right choice.

"Then what?"

"Adventure."

"Adventure?" he repeats.

I take a second and look at him closer. I think I recognize him from somewhere, but I'm not sure. "Yes. Adventure. Let's leave it at that."

"What's your name?" he asks.

"Brooke. And you?" I ask.

"Brandon," he replies.

"Brandon Murphy." I know exactly who he is now.

"The one and only," he says.

"What is a famous drummer doing in Amalfi?" I ask. Brandon Murphy is the drummer from The Talons, a huge band from the UK. They've been on hiatus since finishing a tour they had to postpone the year before.

"Probably the same thing as you, I reckon."

"What's that?"

"Escaping something." He shrugs.

"What are you escaping?" I ask.

"Ah, so you know who I am but don't know my story?" he asks.

"I don't really follow celebrity gossip. Which model broke your heart?" I roll my eyes.

"Hannah, and she wasn't a model—nor did she intend on breaking my heart." His eyes fill with sadness.

"Did she leave you for another musician?" I ask.

"No, she—she uh—" he stops. "She passed away two years ago."

"I'm so sorry," I say. Now I remember. It was everywhere. I couldn't imagine going through the worst thing a person can go through, but not only that, you're going through it in front of the entire world.

"It's all right. Let's not talk about it," He finishes his drink and motions to the server for another.

"Okay."

"If you could also not pity me, that'd be great. I'm tired of people looking at me with sad eyes."

"Sad eyes? What's that?" I tilt my head.

"You know," he makes his eyes a little wider and frowns, looking as sad as possible. I burst out laughing, and he joins me.

"I see what you mean now. I promise I won't," I say. "How long have you been here?"

"Six months," he says. "You're not a fan of The Talons, ay?"

"Not really."

"That's kind of nice. I'm used to people falling all over themselves to talk to me." He takes a sip of his drink, and I copy the motion. The scotch is going down smoother with every drop. "So, what are you going to do now that you're here and have no boyfriend?"

"Uhm—well, I have a job at one of the schools teaching English. Back home, I'm a music teacher," I say.

"Music teacher who doesn't like The Talons. What is wrong with you, love?" he teases. His English accent is less posh than Jessie's husband, Ben.

"I like classical music." I smile.

"Fair enough. How old are you?"

"Twenty-seven. You?" It's like we're playing a game of twenty questions, getting all of the basics out of the way.

"Just turned twenty-five."

"Do you miss London?" I ask.

"Do you miss…" he stops.

"Seattle." I finish.

"Do you miss Seattle?" he asks.

A server carrying a pizza with fresh basil walks by us. The smell of tomato sauce and mozzarella engulf my senses, causes my mouth to water a bit, distracting me from our conversation.

"Earth to Brooke." Brandon snaps his fingers. "Do you miss Seattle?"

"Sorry. Pizza always distracts me." I smile. "I've only been gone a day."

"I miss London," he admits. "I mostly miss my mates."

"Your band?" I ask.

"Yeah, and others. Mick is still in the honeymoon phase even though it's been like a year since they got married," he says. "I was his best man."

"To Candice Bryan?" I ask.

"Right. I thought you didn't follow my band?" His eyes are glimmering. This guy is seriously sexy. It's not even his looks. It's his entire personality.

"I'm guilty of picking up a tabloid or two." I shrug.

"Me too." He winks.

"I'm sure you do." I giggle.

"I miss my friend Knox and Caroline too. They're one-year-old son, Henry is my Godson."

"Knox Bryan and Caroline Harper-Bryan."

"Right again. Sheesh, you're good."

"I only know the names, and I also like The Hestons."

"I'll let Knox know." He smiles.

We continue to talk for another hour before I look down at my watch. The café is starting to get busy with the night rush. In the States, dinner places are busy from five on, but here it's more dinner starts a nine.

"I should get going. Still shaking off the jetlag," I say.

"Yeah. I'll walk with you." He puts down money for the bill.

"Sure." I nod and put on my jacket.

The air has a slight chill. For August, it's a bit colder than normal. As we walk down the streets of Amalfi Town, I point out every restaurant, gelateria and pizzeria that are my favourites and what makes each of them great.

"You act like I haven't been to all these places," he says.

"I forgot that you've been here for the past six months." I blush.

"I like hearing your take on things, though." He smiles.

"Good," I laugh. We fall into a comfortable rhythm as if we've been friends forever. Though his life outside of here is undoubtedly wild, his personality is so calm. It relaxes me. We get to my place, and I turn to him as his face lights up.

"Looks like we're neighbours," he says.

"Actually?" I stop.

"I live at the top of those stairs, and if you live right here then…" He points up at the apartment above mine.

"We're neighbours," I say.

"Guess you should get used to this gorgeous face," he grins.

"Don't threaten me." I roll my eyes.

"When do you start work?" he asks.

"In a month." I sigh. I had come early to spend time with Angelo like we had in the past—adventure and sex.

"If you don't have any plans tomorrow do you want to hang out?" he asks.

"Sure, what do you want to do?" I say. There are worse ways to spend time than with a handsome rock star.

"I'm not sure." His brows furrow.

"Have you been to Positano yet?" I ask

"No..."

"Ravello?"

"No..."

"Pantone?"

"Nope."

"Capri?"

"Let's just say I've been nowhere except Amalfi Town." He scratches the back of his head.

"You haven't gone exploring at all in six months? Have you even been to Rome?" This is insanity to me. He's missing out on some of the most gorgeous places in the world. Sure, Amalfi is stunning, but there's so much more out there.

"Roma, I believe, is the Italian term." He grins. "And yes, I have. I was there a few times with the lads."

"Have you ever explored Rome err—Roma?" I say, correcting myself before he could.

"I've been to the Vatican and the Coliseum."

"What about the Trevi Fountain?"

He shakes his head.

"You're hopeless. Have you been to Florence? Siena? Volterra?" This is unacceptable. This man with endless money has a chance to see everything he could ever want, but he hasn't.

"No. When did this turn into an interrogation about where I've been in Italy?" He chuckles. "Are you disappointed in me?"

"Extremely," I say.

"How am I going to live? The stranger I met because she got dumped in a café a few hours ago, who happens to be my neighbour, is disappointed in me. I am gutted." He clutches his chest.

"You should be. You should also be ashamed of missing everything beautiful that this country has to offer," I say as I turn the lock on my door.

"So I'll see you tomorrow then?" he asks before I duck inside.

"I'll have to think about it now that I know you aren't the brightest," I shut my door. I lean against it and smile. This might not be so bad.

PRE-ORDER BRANDON AND BROOKE'S STORY HERE.

ALSO BY POPPY FORBES

THE TALONS SERIES

1. *Seducing the Rock Star's Sister*
2. *The Rock Star's Happily Ever After*
3. *Healing the Rock Star's Heart*

ACKNOWLEDGMENTS

This will be brief even though I have so many people to mention!

First, my mom, I don't know where I'd be without your encouragement. Thank you to my dad and my brother as well, for even though you don't read these books, you support means a lot.

To my friends who always support all of my crazy ideas, I love you. Thank you for being a part of the journey!

Thank you to Nathalie, of Raven's Publicity for keeping me on the straight and narrow and handling all the things I could never have done without your guidance!

Thank you Jenny Sliger! You have been a great editor and such a joy to work with!

Thank you to my cover designer Sarah Kil, for the absolutely amazing job on this cover and all the others for this series!

Thank you Carmen Richter for formatting! I am in your debt!

Thank you to my ARCs team for reading this book before it was completely edited and being a part of this book!

And thank you to you, the reader, because without you, I wouldn't be able to do what I love!

ABOUT THE AUTHOR

Poppy Forbes is a debut author who specializes in bad boys and the spectacular women who love them. Her debut is a contemporary romance titled *Seducing the Rock Star's Sister*. She loves RomComs, hanging out with her dog, and supporting the romance writer community.

You can find Poppy online here:

Website:

www.poppyforbesauthor.com

Facebook:

wwwfacebook.com/poppyforbesauthor

Instagram:

www.instagram.com/poppyforbesauthor

Amazon:

https://bit.ly/PoppyForbesAmazon

Goodreads:

https://bit.ly/PoppyForbesGR